# Our Next-Door Neighbors

# Our Next-Door Neighbors

## Belle K. Maniates

Original Illustrations by Tony Sarg

Introduction by Patricia Oman

Hastings College Press | Hastings, Nebraska

**Production Staff**

Dakota Anderson

Emilie Barnes

Kaitlyn Baucom

Allie Belitz

Hannah Currey

Razvan Dobrin

Kaitlin Grode

Rachel Jesske

Alex Kreikemeier

Brooke MacLeod

Holly Wolfe

ISBN-10: 1942885164
ISBN-13: 978-1-942885-16-0

Note on the text: This edition has been reset from the first (1917) edition. Original spelling and grammatical conventions have been maintained, except in the case of publishing errors in the first edition. The original punctuation has been maintained but updated using modern conventions (e.g., eliminating spaces around dashes).

# Contents

# Introduction

**Patricia Oman**

When I first discovered the delightful novel *Our Next-Door Neighbors* a few summers ago in a used bookstore, I had never heard of its author. After searching scholarly sources and the Internet, I learned almost nothing about her. It seems that very few people today have heard of Belle K. Maniates. The book in your hands is the first step in correcting that.

Belle Kanaris Maniates was born in 1860 in Marshall, Michigan, the youngest child of Nicholas and Martha Maniates. Despite her current obscurity, she was a writer of some popularity in the early decades of the twentieth century, publishing hundreds of short stories and eight books. *Our Next-Door Neighbors*, her fifth novel, was published in 1917 by Little, Brown & Company, with 55 illustrations by Tony Sarg.

While Maniates spent two decades writing short stories, the success of her second novel, *Amarilly of Clothes-Line Alley* (1915), encouraged her to focus exclusively on novels. She specialized in humorous and sentimental novels about young people that included romantic entanglements, comic misunderstandings, and outrageous plot twists. Although many of her novels center on a plucky young girl (somewhat in the style of Eleanor H. Porter's *Pollyanna*), *Our Next-Door Neighbors* follows the comic story of Lucien and Silvia Wade, a young couple who have been married for 10 years and have built a home in a "small, thriving mid-Western city" (3). Unfortunately for Lucien, the narrator, Silvia is not interested in having children. The wild Polydore children, who move in next door, do not help the situation any. The novel follows the frustrated Wades as they try (unsuccessfully) to evade their young neighbors: the wise and independent Ptolemy, the

Ads for several novels, *New York Times*, 10 March, 1917.

wild Them Three (Pythagoras, Emerald, and Demetrius), and the toddler Diogenes.

Maniates' novels were populist in nature and often involved children, with one reviewer commenting that her style was fun but not "literary" ("A Lovely Love Story"). Contemporaneous newspaper advertisements for *Our Next-Door Neighbors*, for instance, make clear that her publishers were trying to reach a popular audience. One such advertisement described it as a "Rollicking novel" and "A lively comedy, with many a chuckle for the reader, that shows the same sure touch in depicting genuine children that made the author's previous books so popular" ("Our Next-Door Neighbors"). It was frequently advertised alongside another novel from Little, Brown & Company called *Limpy: The Boy Who Felt Neglected*, by William Johnston. As one might guess from the title, this sentimental novel was designed to pull at the readers' heartstrings. Like *Limpy*, *Our Next-Door Neighbors* involves abandoned children, suggesting that Little, Brown & Company was taking advantage of continuing public interest in what Jerry Griswold calls the American orphan "Ur-story." Other, more famous, examples include Mark Twain's *The Adventures of Tom Sawyer* (1876), L. Frank Baum's *The Wonderful Wizard of Oz* (1900), and *Pollyanna* (1913).

*Our Next-Door Neighbors* does, in fact, follow the basic pattern of Griswold's "Ur-story," which starts with a young well-to-do orphan somehow being separated from his parents. Griswold argues, "The hero then makes a journey to another place and is adopted into a second family. In these new circumstances the child is treated harshly by an adult guardian of the same sex but sometimes has help from an adult of the opposite sex. Eventually, however, the child triumphs over its antagonist and is acknowledged" (4). This is exactly what happens to the Polydore children, who have been abandoned by their brilliant but absent-minded parents. The Wades reluctantly take in the children, and the boys clash most frequently with Lucien, who has no idea how to discipline them. (Silvia becomes quite attached to the youngest, Diogenes.) Eventually, however, the boys work their way into Lucien's heart and the second family is complete.

The novel is not just an unoriginal recapitulation of a tired theme, however. Carol J. Singley argues that these adoption narratives are so common in American culture because they reflect the "American migratory experience," specifically that they "reflect politically and culturally the severed ties to Great Britain and the construction of new forms of social and governmental organization" (4). As a result, she argues, "Adoption is a narrative event or trope through which … authors address, often with ambivalence, an evolving American character and nationhood" (4). This ambivalence is certainly visible in *Our Next-Door Neighbors*. The orphaned Polydore children serve as literary devices for expressing ambivalences about shifting and unstable social mores of early twentieth-century America. In fact, despite belonging to a popular (that is, not "literary") genre of literature, the novel is highly critical of a number of mainstream cultural assumptions. The Midwest in this novel serves as the generic location for that critique.

## American Boys and American Men

Claudia Nelson argues that American orphan stories became increasingly sentimental in the early twentieth century. In fact, she argues that there were three distinct periods of orphan stories: "an early period ending about 1890, in which children … are presented primarily in terms of their relation to work; a middle period lasting until about 1914, in which orphans regenerate adults emotionally but both adults and orphans continue to think in terms of practical work; and a late period in which the child's needs are considered paramount" (54). In other words, Nelson tracks a change in conceptions of childhood in American orphan stories from utility to sentiment.

Because *Our Next-Door Neighbors* balances the growing love of the Wades for the Polydore children with the economic benefits they bring, the novel clearly falls into what Nelson calls the "middle period." But, the novel seems uncertain about the exact purpose of the Polydore children—should they provide economic or sentimental value? And how? The novel's ambivalences about the boys' education, class, and future professions reflect changing attitudes and concerns about childhood, especially the rearing of young American boys in the early twentieth century. It therefore draws on two separate types of boy orphans in American literature: the boys-will-be-boys orphan common in Mark Twain's novels (that is, Tom Sawyer and Huck Finn) and the more genteel, thoughtful orphan in novels such as Frances Hodgson Burnett's 1886 novel *Little Lord Fauntleroy*.

In a highly unlikely plot twist, for instance, the mischievous Them Three manage to make Silvia and Lucien a great deal of money, but they do not accomplish this through the traditional definition of work. Through a series of not-so-white lies and boyish pranks, they convince Silvia's wealthy uncle Issachar not only that they are Silvia and Lucien's biological children but that he should make good on his promise to bestow on the Wades $5,000 for each of their children. This episode thus shows the boys' business ingenuity (à la Huck Finn and Tom Sawyer), but the money is still essentially a gift from a wealthy patron.

While Ptolemy has Huck Finn's capacity for compassion, however, he is ultimately more similar to the character Cedric Errol in *Little Lord Fauntleroy*. Burnett's novel was extremely popular and follows a young American boy who learns that his deceased father was actually the son of an English earl. His aristocratic grandfather disowned Cedric's father for marrying an American woman but is impressed with Cedric's innocent and compassionate nature. Eventually he mends his relationship with Cedric's mother. Like Cedric, Ptolemy has a natural ability for compassion and empathy and takes seriously his responsibility to his younger brothers. He also has access to his parents' sizable bank account, which suggests that he, like Cedric, is actually a member of the upper class. Uncle Issachar's gift to the family is thus similar to the earl's acceptance of both Cedric and his American mother. Just as Cedric's grandfather rewards his daughter-in-law for bringing up Cedric so well, Uncle Issachar rewards Silvia for raising her sons "up fine" (152). This plot contrivance is a comedy of errors in the style of Mark Twain, but the result is the settling of an aristocratic inheritance.

Uncle Issachar believes that boys should not be "mollycoddles or Lizzie boys" (152) and tells Silvia "he didn't suppose [they] had so much sense as to leave them natural" (152). But, when the Wades formally decide to adopt the children, they debate the best way to educate them—send them to public school or a boys' military school? Even though the maid Huldah astutely comments, "'If Them Three ever meets that there Viller man … the fur will fly some'" (172), no one likes the idea of the boys eventually being "ordered to Mexico to protect us" (172). Further, when Lucien and his friend Rob Rossiter debate the best profession for Ptolemy, they consider only middle-class, white-collar professions: business or law. Given the similarity of the younger Polydore children to Twain's young rascals, Huck Finn and Tom Sawyer, the suggestion that they will eventually be "sivilized" (as Huck calls it) seems unlikely, however.

While *Our Next-Door Neighbors* celebrates the "bad boy" vein of American children's literature, it is ambivalent about the hypermasculinity espoused by early twentieth-century public figures such as Theodore Roosevelt. In a 1900 essay called "The American Boy," for instance, Roosevelt argues that an American boy "must not be a coward or a weakling, a bully, a shirk, or a prig. He must work hard and play hard. He must be clean-minded and clean-lived, and be able to hold his own under all circumstances and against all comers" (155). This description certainly applies to the Polydore boys, who excel at playing and working hard and who prove to be big-hearted, but Maniates does not seem to approve of the subtext for this argument. At the beginning of this essay, Roosevelt argues that an active boyhood will create "the kind of American man of whom America can be really proud" (155). But his first concrete example shows that he is really talking about the ideal way to create good soldiers:

> In the Civil War the soldiers who came from the prairie and the backwoods and the rugged farms where stumps still dotted the clearings, and who had learned to ride in their infancy, to shoot as soon as they could handle a rifle, and to camp out whenever they got the chance, were better fitted for military work than any set of mere school or college athletes could be. (156–57)

While *Our Next-Door Neighbors* is full of boys-will-be-boys humor, it does not buy into the military rhetoric of the early twentieth century. Despite the Polydore boys' aptitude for outdoor pursuits and the likelihood that they would be excellent soldiers, the Wades do not allow it.

Having been born right before the Civil War, Maniates was probably aware of the effects of war on men who return home and on the families they leave behind. In fact, for a few years she served as the Chief of the Widow Department at the U.S. Pension Office in Detroit and then worked for over 20 years as a clerk in the Michigan Adjutant General's Office. Her career, therefore, would have put her in continuous contact with military veterans and their families. Her authorial unwillingness to send even the wild Polydore boys off to military school may have been influenced by this contact.

## Womanly Women and Manly Men

In addition to hedging about early twentieth-century America's assumptions about rearing boys, *Our Next-Door Neighbors* questions the normative gender roles of the Wades.

Silvia, for instance, is presented by her husband (the narrator) as a slight aberration, a woman who is not interested in being a mother. Lucien attributes the fact that they do not have children after 10 years of marriage to his wife's unnatural dislike of children, explaining to the reader, "I had hoped that her understanding and love for children might be developed in the usual and natural way, but we had now been married ten years and this hope had not been realized" (4). His argument that his wife does not follow "the usual and natural way" suggests that he expects a woman of this time to want children.

As one might expect, Silvia's character development includes learning to be maternal toward the wild Polydore children, but Lucien also undergoes a shift toward more normative gender roles when he learns to be stricter as a father. In fact, while the children spontaneously start calling Silvia "mudder," they refer to Lucien as "stepdaddy" and generally disregard his commands. Despite their wild behavior, Lucien is reluctant to discipline them at all. In one early episode he comes close but quickly loses his nerve:

> Polydore proclivities made the Reign of Terror
> formerly known as the French Revolution seem
> like an ice-cream festival. I don't regard myself as a
> particularly nervous man, but there's a limit! Their
> war whoops and screeches got on my nerves and
> temper to the extent of sending me into their midst
> one evening brandishing a whip and commanding
> immediate silence. I got it. Not through fear of
> chastisement, for fear was an emotion unknown to a
> Polydore, but from astonishment at so unexpected a
> procedure from so unexpected a source. Heretofore I
> had either ignored them or frolicked with them. (36)

Rather than carrying out the threat, however, Lucien backs out of the room leaving them to continue their racket. Lucien, therefore, has to learn how to be a father, not "stepdaddy" or a pal. When he finally begins disciplining the children, spanking

Diogenes for jumping out of a window and denying Pythagoras a baseball game for spying, the children finally start to behave.

The models for these normative gender roles are Lucien's sister Beth and his old college chum Rob. While Silvia and Lucien try to avoid the Polydores whenever possible, Beth and Rob like spending time with them, Beth baking for them and Rob playing sports and camping with them. Beth and Rob's inevitable courtship is delayed only by Rob's assumption that Beth is "the new woman type" (80), which he describes as "strong-minded and a man-hater" (99). The "New Woman" was a term used in the late nineteenth and early twentieth centuries to refer to a woman who was independent and often had a career. Today, we might substitute the word "feminist." New Women went to college and rode bicycles. They wrote plays and wore trousers rather than skirts. Sometimes they were overtly political, advocating for women's suffrage. Beth strenuously denies this accusation and accepts Rob's proposal for marriage once Lucien assures her that Rob is "a man's man" (98). The novel thus makes clear the proper gender roles of a nuclear family and suggests that the Polydore children can be tamed only by parents who perform their proper roles.

The novel is ultimately ambivalent about normative gender roles, however. The most criticized character of the novel is Mrs. Polydore, a woman too absorbed in her research and writing on antiquities to spend any time with her children. Lucien describes her face as "angular" and "sharp-cut" with the "form of a rocking horse" (13), suggesting that she is a hard, unattractive woman. Another character, the young female reporter Miss Frayne, describes her as "an untidy, disheveled-looking woman" despite recognizing in her absorption "the same breathless way I write when I have a scoop, and the presses are waiting open-mouthed for my copy" (129–30). Miss Frayne's admiration for Mrs. Polydore's work does not absolve the children's mother for her lack of maternal interest or femininity, however. As Rob notes, despite Miss Frayne's professional talents, she will quit her job when she marries Rob's cousin. Or at least Rob seems to think so. While the novel is generally critical of women who refuse expected gender norms by not wanting children, not projecting feminine beauty standards, or wanting a career, Mrs. Polydore is actually similar to Maniates herself. Both women could be called "New Women."

Belle Maniates never married and never had children. She supported herself her entire adult life, retiring in 1923 or 1924, when she was in her 60s. In other words, Maniates focused on her career and writing. The sheer volume of fiction she produced—hundreds of short stories and eight books—suggests that she, like Mrs. Polydore, was "mad about writing" (139). Despite the novel's seeming approval of normative gender roles, therefore, there are disruptive moments that question them. Ptolemy, for instance, defends his mother from the criticisms of the Wades by explaining, "If she sees a blank paper anywhere, she ain't happy until she has written something on it, and the sight of a pencil makes her fingers itch" (139). In other words, he argues that his mother cannot help her absorption in her work. Implicitly Ptolemy may also be defending Silvia for her lack of maternal instinct. The novel's criticisms of Silvia for not wanting children and of Mrs. Polydore for being absorbed in her work thus point to a complicated relationship between the author and the subject of *Our Next-Door Neighbors*. Why would Maniates criticize the New Woman when, whether by choice or circumstances, she was one?

Perhaps we can attribute the novel's ambivalences about gender roles to the narrator himself. Although the first-person narration seems uncomplicated and Lucien an authoritative narrator, most of the novel's critiques of non-normative gender behavior are mediated through his voice. In other words, the novel critiques women who do not conform to expected gender norms because it is told from Lucien's perspective. The two characters who have sympathy for Mrs. Polydore, Miss Frayne and the young Ptolemy, are voices from the margin who might be expected to defy those norms. Despite his growing awareness of his own faults, therefore, Lucien could also be read as an unreliable narrator. That is, perhaps Maniates wrote the story from the perspective of an educated, white, middle-class man to demonstrate that normative gender roles are the product of this subject position. This reading makes sense when compared to Maniates' other novels, which (with the exception of her first novel, *David Dunne: A Romance of the Middle West*) focus on young, independent women rather than middle-class men. The choice to have Lucien narrate the story is also unusual within the context of American orphan stories, which always focus on the orphan as the protagonist. *Our Next-Door Neighbors* is really about Lucien and Silvia.

## Middle-Class Consumer Aspirations and the Cult of Domesticity

The orphan theme in *Our Next-Door Neighbors* does not apply just to the Polydore children. Lucien implies that Silvia herself had been an orphan as a child, arguing, "Her upcoming had been supervised by a grimalkin governess who drew around the form of her young charge the awful circle of exclusiveness, intercourse with children being strictly prohibited" (1). The emphasis on the governess rather than a mother implies that Silvia was a virtual orphan with no doting mother to provide affection. In fact, Lucien even argues, "She grew up an outlawed, isolated child" with "the handicaps of so barren a childhood" (3). This is an interesting twist on Griswold's orphan "Ur-story" because Silvia's marriage to Lucien is like the orphan's "Second Life." Her reluctance to become a mother could be a function of the cultural ambivalence inherent to American adoption narratives.

In fact, Silvia's role as an orphan points to shifting cultural assumptions about the role of the mother in middle-class families in the early twentieth century, a transformation from the "angel" of the home at the center of the Victorian "cult of domesticity" to the scientific "homemaker" of the twentieth century. Lucien bemoans the fact that his wife is not motherly, arguing, "She had tried most assiduously to cultivate an acquaintance with members of child-world, but into that kingdom there is no open sesame. The sure keen intuition of a child recognizes on sight a kindred spirit and Silvia's forced advances met with but indifferent responses" (4). And yet, he argues that "Silvia had all the requisites of mind and manner and Domestic Science necessary to a 'hearth- and home-' maker" (3). The phrase "Domestic Science" refers to the burgeoning field of Home Economics, which started in the later nineteenth century but took off in the early twentieth. Silvia's inability to connect with children could be a critique of the academic/scientific nature of the movement.

The field of home economics was pushed to the forefront of American consciousness and politics by a growing movement that eventually helped to establish it as a regular course in land-grant universities and rural areas through the Smith-Lever Act of 1914 and the Smith-Hughes Act of 1917. Lucien's phrase "hearth and home" comes directly from one of the first "domestic science" magazines, *Hearth and Home*, which ran weekly from 1868 to 1876. Despite the ubiquity of sentimental-sounding publications aimed at improving American domestic life, however, there was a major shift in philosophy around the turn of the century. As Kathleen Anne McHugh argues, in the early decades of the twentieth century, "The prevailing social ethos shifted from an emphasis on a superior, feminized otherworldliness and sentimentality to one that espoused the values of science, objectivity, and progress" (60). She writes further, "Referred to as 'domestic engineering' or 'household management,' this new approach applied Frederick Winslow Taylor's efficiency methods and Frank Gilbreth's time and motion studies to the performance of housework" (61). Thus, whereas the Victorian cult of domesticity emphasized the "subjective, emotional, and spiritual, … [d]omestic engineers … promoted the objective authority of science, of the expert, and of rational, calculated housekeeping methods that guaranteed results for all" (61). Lucien's association of Silvia with "Domestic Science" is thus a double-edged sword. It may have taught her the fashionable way to run a middle-class family, but it turned her away from the Victorian "cult of domesticity" that Lucien desires.

The novel (or at least, Lucien) suggests that there is something barren about the comfortable middle-class life that the Wades live. In fact, his description of their house as "one of many made to the same measure with the inevitable street porch, big window, trimmed lawn in front and garden in rear" (3) indicates that they have settled into a cookie-cutter life defined by middle-class expectations rather than by themselves. In fact, Lucien acknowledges this when he explains, "We had attained the standard of prosperity maintained in our home town by keeping 'hired help' and installing a telephone, so our social status was fixed" (3). They are not happy with this level of "prosperity," however, constantly worrying about how they will afford the trappings of an even more affluent lifestyle: a piano, a horse, and a car.

The Wades' interest in consumer culture is not unusual at this time, however. In fact, Carolyn M. Goldstein argues that consumerism was actually an important part of home economics in the early twentieth century. Increased industrialization brought about changes in the production of goods used in the home, which meant that middle-class home economists could now buy many of the items they used to make at home, such as soap, bread, canned goods, and packaged meats (Goldstein 23–24). As a good home economist, Silvia is not careless with money, but her middle-class desire for material objects is always present.

An article by Mildred Maddocks in the January 1917 issue of *Good Housekeeping* exemplifies the early twentieth-century focus on creating the ideal middle-class home, describing how newly married couples could set up their houses tastefully but cheaply:

> In order to make the experiment practical for any
> section of the country the equipping was done
> in every detail from nationally distributed goods:
> furniture, silver, china, and kitchen-ware can all
> be purchased in the smallest towns as well as in
> New York.... The entire cost will vary but little
> throughout the country and need never exceed $400
> for all of the furniture required for five rooms, the
> linen, both bed and table, the silver, glassware, china,

cooking-utensils, and laundry appliances. Only the
range and refrigerator—both of which are frequently
rented—are omitted from the estimate. (72)

The assumption that newlyweds will spend $400 on house
furnishings in 1917 indicates that this article is aimed at a
securely middle-class audience. Adjusted for inflation, for
instance, $400 in 1917 would be about $8,000 today. The list
of necessary items—including silver and china—also indicates
the lifestyle to which the magazine assumes subscribers aspire.
The fact that all of these items are "nationally distributed goods"
means not only that anyone (with $400) can achieve a model
home, but that consumers are encouraged to create the *same*
home. In fact, Maddocks' advice about what colors would work
best with this furniture encourages blandness: "In order to make
an inexpensively furnished home distinctive, the color-scheme
must be good, but very simple. Adopt one neutral color for all
room papers. In this case gray was chosen of the softer brown cast
rather than the blue" (72). Her recommendation for "one neutral
color" hardly seems "distinctive."

Elsewhere in the article, Maddocks mentions that the home
is "presided over by a capable colored maid who takes very kindly
to the latest tools and methods and the new cook-books that are
subtly placed in her way" (72). This clarification informs readers
not only that they should desire to be wealthy enough to have
hired help, not only that they should buy all of the latest kitchen
gadgets, but also that they should be open to "the latest tools
and methods." In other words, Maddocks signals to readers that
this "experiment" is an exercise in the scientific field of home
economics, even though to today's readers it might look more like
a page from an Ikea catalog.

Significantly, this article, which was published only a
month before *Our Next-Door Neighbors*, describes the Wade
household almost perfectly. Silvia, for instance, is so angry she
can hardly speak when she catches Ptolemy using one of her
china soup bowls to carry live fishing bait. And Huldah actually
does all of the housework for Silvia, even taking care of Them

Three when the Wades go on vacation. The Polydore children are thus a powerful challenge to the Wades' antiseptic, middle-class life. Eventually they are able to pull Silvia away from her love of things to more maternal feelings. In fact, when the elder Polydores skip town and leave their children with the Wades, Silvia is at first attracted by the blank check their father leaves. Lucien intervenes, however, saying, "No, Silvia … not for any number of blank checks or vacation trips shall you have the care and annoyance of those wild Comanches" (34). His description of the Polydore boys as American Indians is obviously supposed to be humorous, but the implication of wildness suggests that the Wades consider the boys a disruption of their comfortable middle-class lifestyle.

When the youngest, Diogenes, becomes ill just a few hours later, however, Silvia's maternal instinct kicks in and she refuses to pawn off the children on a hired caregiver. In other words, one sick Polydore turns Silvia from a cold domestic scientist who values middle-class consumerism to the sentimental "angel" of the Victorian American family. The fact that Sylvia and Lucien both have to reject some of the principles of middle-class life that they have learned from mass culture to be good parents suggests that the picture of middle-class life advocated by popular magazines such as *Good Housekeeping* is not actually conducive to good parenting.

While not overtly subversive, *Our Next-Door Neighbors* does raise several questions about early twentieth-century America. Does a married woman have to be a mother? Do young boys have to grow into hypermasculine men? The novel is a reflection of its time, but its time is wildly unsettled. In many ways, the novel straddles the nineteenth and twentieth centuries, insisting that the orphans at the center of the story pay their way while resisting the consumerism and faddishness of early twentieth-century America, reinforcing normative gender roles while leaving open the possibility for women to have careers outside the home, and critiquing the sterility of modern home economics and its emphasis on consumerism while rewarding the newly formed middle-class family with wealth. *Our Next-Door Neighbors* is not just a "Rollicking novel," therefore. It is also a window into a rollicking time in American history.

## Works Cited

Goldstein, Carolyn M. *Creating Consumers: Home Economists in Twentieth-Century America*. Chapel Hill: University of North Carolina Press, 2012. Print.

Griswold, Jerry. *Audacious Kids: Coming of Age in America's Classic Children's Books*. New York: Oxford University Press, 1992. Print.

"A Lovely Love Story." *Reedy's Mirror* XXVII.12 (22 Mar. 1918): 184. *Books.google.com*. Web. 10 June 2015.

Maddocks, Mildred. "What It Costs to Set Up Housekeeping." *Good Housekeeping* 64.1 (Jan. 1917): 72–73. *Hearth.library. cornell.edu*. Web. 15 June 2015.

Maniates, Belle. *Our Next-Door Neighbors*. Hastings, NE: Hastings College Press, 2015 [1917].

McHugh, Kathleen Anne. *American Domesticity: From How-to-Manual to Hollywood Melodrama*. Cary, NC: Oxford University Press, 1999. *ProQuest ebrary*. Web. 4 Aug. 2015.

Nelson, Claudia. "Drying the Orphan's Tear: Changing Representations of the Dependent Child in America, 1870–1930." *Children's Literature* 29 (2001): 52–70.

"Our Next-Door Neighbors." Advertisement. *New York Times* 10 Mar. 1917: 8. *ProQuest Historical Newspapers*. Web. 27 June 2014.

Roosevelt, Theodore. "The American Boy" in *The Strenuous Life: Essays and Addresses*. New York: The Century Co., 1902. 153–64. Print.

Singley, Carol J. *Adopting America: Childhood, Kinship, and National Identity in Literature*. New York: Oxford University Press, 2011. Print.

**Other Titles by Belle K. Maniates**

*Amarilly of Clothes-Line Alley*. Boston: Little, Brown & Company, 1915.[1]
*Amarilly in Love*. Boston: Little, Brown & Company, 1917.
*David Dunne: A Romance of the Middle West*. Chicago: Rand McNally & Company, 1912.
*Little Boy Bear*. Boston: Pilgrim Press, 1917.
*Mildew Manse*. Boston: Little, Brown & Company, 1916.
*Penny of Top Hill Trail*. Chicago: The Reilly & Lee Company, 1919.
*Sand Holler*. Chicago: The Reilly & Lee Company, 1920.

.............................................

Patricia Oman is Assistant Professor of English at Hastings College and Director of Hastings College Press. She received her PhD in English from the University of Oregon and teaches courses in literature, visual culture, publishing, and writing. Dr. Oman has published articles on a number of American writers—including Willa Cather, Eleanor Porter, Toni Morrison, and Richard Powers—and is currently writing a book on the life and literary career of Belle K. Maniates.

---

[1] New edition forthcoming from Hastings College Press, spring 2016.

# I

## About Silvia and Myself

Some people have children born unto them, some acquire children and others have children thrust upon them. Silvia and I are of the last named class. We have no offspring of our own, but yesterday, today, and forever we have those of our neighbor.

We were born and bred in the same little home-grown city and as a small boy, even, I was Silvia's worshiper, but perforce a worshiper from afar.

Her upcoming had been supervised by a grimalkin governess who drew around the form of her young charge the awful circle of exclusiveness, intercourse with child-kind being strictly prohibited.

Children are naturally gregarious little creatures, however, and Silvia on rare occasions managed to break parole and make adroit escape from surveillance. Then she would speed to the top of the boundary wall that separated the stable precincts from an alluring alley which was the playground of the plebeian progeny of the humble born.

To the circle of dirty but fascinating ragamuffins she became an interested tangent, a silent observer. Here I had my first meeting with her. I was not of her class, neither was I to the alley born, but sailed in the sane mid-channel that ameliorates the distinction between high and low life.

On this eventful day I was taking a short cut on my way to school. One of the group of alleyites, with the inherent friendliness of the unchartered but big-hearted members of the silt of the stream of humans, had proffered to little Silvia a chip on which was a patch of mud designed to become a fruitcake stuffed with pebbles in lieu of raisins and frosted with moistened ashes. Before the enticing pastime of transformation was begun, however, Silvia was swiftly snatched from the contaminating midst and borne away over the ramparts.

Thereafter I haunted the alley, hoping for another glimpse of the little picture girl on the wall. At last I attained my desire. One Saturday afternoon I saw her coming, alone, down a long rosebush bordered path. A thrill ran through me. Our eyes met. Yet all I found to say was: "C'mon over."

She responded to this invitation and I helped her over the wall. She looked longingly at the Irish playing in the mud, but a clean sandpile in my own backyard not far away seemed to me a more fitting environment for one so daintily clad.

We played undisturbed for a never-to-be-forgotten half hour and then they found her out. Reprimanding voices jangled and the whole world was out of tune.

Thereafter a strict watch was kept on little Silvia's movements and I saw her only at rare intervals, when she was going into church or as she rode past our house. She always remembered me and on such meetings a faint, reminiscent smile lighted the somber little face and her eyes met mine as if in a mysterious promise.

She grew up an outlawed, isolated child deprived of her birthright, but in spite of the handicaps of so barren a childhood, she achieved young womanhood unspoiled and in possession of her early democratic tendencies.

When I was making a modest start in a legal way, her parents died and left her with that most unprofitable of legacies, an encumbered estate. Then I dared to renew our acquaintance begun on the sandpile. She went to live with a poor but practical relation and was initiated into the science of stretching an inadequate income to meet everyday needs. In time I wooed and won her.

We set up housekeeping in a small, thriving mid-Western city where I secured a partnership in a legal firm. Silvia had all the requisites of mind and manner and Domestic Science necessary to a "hearth-and home-" maker.

We lived in a house which was one of many made to the same measure with the inevitable street porch, big window, trimmed lawn in front and garden in the rear. We had attained the standard of prosperity maintained in our home town by keeping "hired help" and installing a telephone, so our social status was fixed.

There was but one adjunct missing to our little Arcadia. While at a word or look children flocked to me like friendly puppies in response to a call, to Silvia they were still an unknown quantity.

I had hoped that her understanding and love for children might be developed in the usual and natural way, but we had now been married ten years and this hope had not been realized.

She had tried most assiduously to cultivate an acquaintance with members of child-world, but into that kingdom there is no open sesame. The sure keen intuition of a child recognizes on sight a kindred spirit and Silvia's forced advances met with but indifferent response. She wistfully proposed to me one day that we adopt a child. My doubts as to the advisability of such a course were confirmed by Huldah, our strong staff in household help. In our section of the country servants were generally quite conversant with the intimate and personal affairs of the home.

"Don't you never do it, Mr. Wade," she counseled. "Ready-mades ain't for the likes of her."

When, in acting on this advice, I vetoed Silvia's lukewarm proposition, I was convinced of Huldah's wisdom by seeing the look of relief that flashed into my wife's troubled countenance, and I knew that her suggestion had been but a perfunctory prompting of duty.

Time alone could overcome the effects of her early environment!

# II

# Introducing Our
# Next-Door Neighbors

One morning Silvia and I lingered over our coffee cups discussing our plans for the coming summer, which included visits from my sister Beth and my college chum, Rob Rossiter. We wished to avoid having their arrivals occur simultaneously, however, because Rob was a woman-hater, or thought he was. We decided to have Beth pay her visit first and later take Rob with us on our vacation trip to some place where the fishing facilities would be to our liking. However, summer vacation time like our plans was yet far, vague and dim.

While I was putting on my overcoat, Silvia had gone to the window and was looking pensively at the vacant house next to ours.

"I fear," she said abruptly and irrelevantly, "that we are destined to receive no part of Uncle Issachar's fortune."

Uncle Issachar was a wealthy but eccentric relative of my wife. He had made us no wedding gift beyond his best wishes, but he had then informed us that at the birth of each of our prospective sons he should place in the bank to Silvia's account the sum of five thousand dollars. We had never invited him to visit us or made any overtures in the way of communication with him, lest he should think we were cultivating his acquaintance from mercenary motives.

While I was debating whether the lament in Silvia's tone was for the loss of the money or the lack of children, she again spoke; this time in a tone which had lost its languor.

"There is a big moving van in front of the house next door. At last we will have some near neighbors."

"Are they unloading furniture?" I asked inanely, crossing to the window.

"No; course not," came cheerfully from Huldah, who had come in to remove the dishes. "Most likely they are unloading lions and tigers."

As I have already intimated, Huldah was a privileged servant.

"They are unloading children!" explained Silvia, in a tone implying that Huldah's sarcastic implication would be infinitely more preferable. "The van seems to be overflowing with them—a perfect crowd. Do you suppose the house is to be used as an orphan asylum?"

"I think not," I assured her as I counted the flock. Five children would seem like a crowd to Silvia.

"Boys!" exclaimed Huldah tragically, as she joined us for a survey. "I'll see that they don't keep the grass off our lawn."

Late that afternoon I opened the outer door of the dining-room in response to the rap of strenuously applied knuckles.

A lad of about eleven years with the sardonic face of a satyr and diabolically bright eyes peered into the room.

"We're going to have soup for dinner," he announced, "and mother wants to borrow a soup plate for father to eat his out of."

Silvia stared at him aghast. She seemed to feel something compelling in the boy's person, however, and she went to the china closet and brought forth a soup plate which she handed to him without comment.

In silence we watched him run across the lawn, twirling the plate deftly above his head in juggler fashion.

The next day when we sat down to dinner our new young neighbor again appeared on our threshold.

"Halloa!" he called chummily. "We are going to have soup again and we want a soup plate for father."

"Where is the one I loaned you yesterday?" demanded Silvia in a tone far below thirty-two degrees Fahrenheit, while her features assumed a frigidity that would have congealed father's favorite sustenance had it been in her vicinity.

"Oh, we broke that!" he casually and cheerfully explained.

With much reluctance Silvia bestowed another plate upon the young applicant.

"Wait!" I said as he started to leave, "don't you want the soup tureen, too, or the ladle and some soup spoons?"

"No, thank you," he answered politely. "None of the rest of us like soup, so we dish father's up in the kitchen. He doesn't like soup particularly, but he eats it because it goes down quick and lets him have more time for work."

This time as he sped homeward, he didn't spin the plate in air, but tried out a new plan of balancing it on a stick.

"I think," I suggested gently, when our young neighbor was lost to our sorrowful sight, "that it might be well to invest in another dozen or so of soup plates. I will see about getting them at wholesale rates. Our supply will soon give out if our new neighbors continue to cultivate the soup and borrowing habit."

"I will buy some at the five cent store," replied Silvia. "I think I had better call upon them tomorrow and see what manner of people they can be."

When I came home the next day it was quite evident that she had called.

"Well," I inquired, "what do they keep—a soup house?"

"They are literary people, the highest of high-brows. Their name is Polydore, and the head of the house—"

"Mr. or Mrs.?" I interrupted.

"The head of the house," pursued Silvia, ignoring my question, "is a collector."

"So I inferred. Has he a large collection of soup plates?"

"She collects antiquities and writes their history. He pursues science."

"They were seemingly communicative. What did they look like?"

"I didn't see them. After I rang I heard a woman's voice bidding some one not to answer the bell. She said she couldn't be bothered with interruptions, so I went on up the street to call on Mrs. Fleming, who told me all about them. She was also refused admittance when she called. On my way home I met that boy—that awful boy—"

She paused, evidently overcome by the consideration of his awfulness.

"He had been digging bait—"

Again she paused as if words were inadequate for her climax.

"Well," I encouraged.

"He was carrying his bait—horrid, wriggling angleworms—in our soup plate!"

"Then it is not broken yet!" I exclaimed joyfully. "Let us hope it is given an antiseptic bath before father's next indulgence in consommé. After dinner I will go over and try my luck at paying my respects to the soup savant."

"They won't let you in."

"In that case I shall follow their lead of setting aside all ceremony and formality and admit myself, as their heir apparent does here."

After dinner and my twilight smoke, I went next door, first asking Silvia if there was anything we needed that I could borrow, just to show them there were no hard feelings.

My third vigorous ring brought results. A slipshod servant appeared and reluctantly seated me in the hall. She read with seeming interest the card I handed to her and then, pushing aside some mangy-looking portières, vanished from view.

She evidently delivered my card, for I heard a woman's voice read my name, "Mr. Lucien Wade."

After another short interval the slovenly servant returned and offered me my card.

"She seen it," she assured me in answer to my look of surprise.

She again put the portières between us, and I was obliged to own myself baffled in my efforts to break in. I was showing myself out when my onward course was deflected by a troop of noisy children headed by the soup plate skirmisher, who was the oldest and apparently the leader of the brood.

"Oh, halloa!" he greeted me with the air of an old acquaintance, "didn't you see the folks?"

On my informing him that I had seen no one but the servant, he exclaimed:

"Oh, that chicken wouldn't know enough to ask you in! Just follow us. Mother wouldn't remember to come out."

I was loath to force my presence on mother, but by this time my hospitable young friend had pulled the portières so strenuously that they parted from the pole, and I was presented willy nilly to the collector of antiquities, who had the angular sharp-cut face and form of a rocking horse. She was seated at a table strewn with books and papers, writing at a rate of speed that convinced me she was in the throes of an inspiration. I forebore to interrupt. My scruples, however, were not shared by her eldest son. He gave her elbow a jog of reminder which sent her pencil to the floor.

"Mother!" he shouted in megaphone voice, "here's the man next door—the one we get our soup plates from."

She looked up abstractedly.

"Oh," she said in dismayed tone, "I thought you had gone. I am very much engaged in writing a paper on modern antiquities."

I murmured some sort of an apology for my untimely interruption.

"I am so absorbed in my great work," she explained, "that I am oblivious to all else. I have the rare and great gift of concentration in a marked degree."

I was quite sure of this fact. She took another pencil from a supply box and resumed her literary occupation. As my presence seemed of so little moment, I lingered.

"Mother," shouted one of the boys, snatching the pencil from her grasp, "I'm hungry. I didn't have any supper."

"Yes, you did!" she asserted. "I saw Gladys give you a bowl of bread and milk."

"Emerald took it away from me and drank it up."

"Didn't neither!" denied a shaggy looking boy. "I spilled it."

He accompanied this denial by a fierce punch in his accuser's ribs.

"Here!" said the author of Modern Antiquities, taking a nickel from her pocket, "go get yourself some popcorn, Demetrius."

"I ain't Demetrius! I'm Pythagoras."

"It makes no difference. Go and get it and don't speak to me again tonight."

The boy had already snatched the coin, and he now started for the exit, but his outgoing way was instantly blocked by a promiscuous pack of pugilistic Polydores, and an ardent and general onslaught followed.

I endeavored to untangle the arms and legs of the attackers and the attacked in a desire to rescue the youngest, a child of two, but I soon beat a retreat, having no mind to become a punching bag for Polydores.

The concentrator at the writing table, looking up vaguely, perceived the general joust.

"How provoking!" she exclaimed indignantly. "I was in search of an antonym and now they've driven it out of my memory."

I politely offered my sympathy for her loss.

"Did you ever see such misbehaved children?" she asked casually and impersonally as she calmly surveyed the free-for-all fight.

"Children always misbehave before company," I remarked propitiatingly. "Of course they know better."

"Why no, they don't!" she declared, looking at me in surprise, "they—"

At this instant the errant antonym evidently flashed upon her mental vision and her pencil hastened to record it, and then flew on at lightning speed.

I was about to try to make an escape when a momentary cessation of hostilities was caused by the entrance of a moth-eaten, abstracted-looking man. As the *two-year-old* hailed him as "fadder," I gathered that he was the person responsible for the family now fighting at his feet.

"What's the trouble?" he asked helplessly.

"She gave Thag a nickel," explained the eldest boy, "and we want it."

The man drew a sigh of relief. The solution of this family problem was instantly and satisfactorily met by an impartial distribution of nickels.

With demoniac whoops of delight, the contestants fled from the room.

I introduced myself to the man of the house, who seemed to realize that some sort of compulsory conventionalities must be observed. He looked hopelessly at his wife, and seeing that she was beyond response to an S O S call to things mundane, he frankly but impressively informed me that I must expect nothing of them socially as their lives were devoted to research and study. The children, however, he assured me, could run over frequently to see us.

I instinctively felt that my call was considered ended, so I took my departure. I related the details of my neighborly visit to Silvia, but her sense of humor was not stirred. It was entirely dominated by her dread of the young Polydores.

"How many children are there?" she asked faintly. "More than the five you said you counted that first day?"

"They seemed not so many as much. That is, though I suppose in round numbers there are but five, yet each of those five is equal to at least three ordinary children."

"Are they all boys? Huldah says the youngest wears dresses."

"Nevertheless he is a boy. They are all unmistakably boys. I think they must have been born with boots on and," conscious of the imprints on my shins, "hobnail boots at that. Even the youngest, a two-year-old, seems to have been graduated from Home Rule."

"I can't bear to think of their going to bed hungry," she said wistfully. "Think of that unnatural mother expecting them to satisfy their hunger by popcorn."

"They didn't though," I assured her. "I saw them stop a street vendor below here and invest their nickels in hot dogs."

"Hot dogs!" repeated Silvia in horror.

"Wienerwursts," I hastened to interpret.

# III

# In Which We Are Pestered
# by Polydores

Our life now became one long round of Polydores. They were with us burr-tight, and attached themselves to me with dog-like devotion, remaining utterly impervious to Silvia's aloofness and repulses. At last, however, she succumbed to their presence as one of the things inevitable.

"The Polydores are here to stay," she acknowledged in a calmness-of-despair voice.

"They don't seem to be homebodies," I allowed.

The children were not literary like the other productions of their profound parents, but were a band of robust, active youngsters unburdened with brains, excepting Ptolemy of soup plate fame. Not that he betrayed any tendencies toward a learned line, but he was possessed of an occult, uncanny, wizard-like wisdom that was disconcerting.

His contemplative eyes seemed to search my soul and read my inmost thoughts.

Pythagoras, Emerald, and Demetrius, aged respectively nine, eight, and seven, were very much alike in looks and size, being so many pinched caricatures of their mother. To Silvia they were bewildering whirlwinds, but Huldah, who seemed to have difficulty in telling them apart, always classified them as "Them three," and Silvia and I fell into the habit of referring to them in the same way. Huldah could not master the Polydore given names either by memory or pronunciation. Ptolemy, whose name was shortened to "Tolly" by Diogenes, she called "Polly." When she was on speaking terms with "Them three" she nicknamed them "Thaggy, Emmy, and Meetie."

Diogenes, the two-year-old, was a Tartar when emulating his brothers. Alone, he was sometimes normal and a shade more like ordinary children.

When they first began swarming in upon us, Silvia drew many lines which, however, the Polydores promptly effaced.

"They shall not eat here, anyway," she emphatically declared.

This was her last stand and she went down ingloriously.

One day while we were seated at the table enjoying some of Huldah's most palatable dishes, Ptolemy came in. There ensued on our part a silence which the lad made no effort to break. Silvia and I each slipped him a side glance. He stood statuesque, watching us with the mute wistfulness of a hungry animal. There were unwonted small red specks

high upon his cheekbones, symptoms, Silvia thought, of
starvation.

She was moved to ask, though reluctantly and
perfunctorily:

"Haven't you been to dinner, Ptolemy?"

"Yes," he admitted quickly, "but I could eat another."

Assuming that the forced inquiry was an invitation,
before protest could be entered he supplied himself with a
plate and helped himself to food. His need and relish of the
meal weakened Silvia's fortifications.

This opening, of course, was the wedge that let in
other Polydores, and thereafter we seldom sat down to a
meal without the presence of one or more members of the
illustrious and famished family, who made themselves as
entirely at home as would a troop of foraging soldiers. Silvia
gazed upon their devouring of food with the same surprised,
shocked, and yet interested manner in which one watches
the feeding of animals.

"I suppose he ought not to eat so many pickles," she
remarked one day, as Emerald consumed his ninth Dill.

"You can't kill a Polydore," I assured her.

I never opened a door but more or less Polydores
fell in. They were at the left of us and at the right of us,
with Diogenes always under foot. We had no privacy.
I found myself waking suddenly in the night with the
uncomfortable feeling that Ptolemy lurked in a dark corner
or two of my bedroom.

Even Silvia's boudoir was not free from their invasion.
But one door in our house remained closed to them. They
found no open sesame to Huldah's apartment.

"I wish she would let me in on her system," I said. "I wonder how she manages to keep them on the outside?"

"I can tell you," confided Silvia. "Emerald and Demetrius went in one day and she dropped Demetrius out the window and kicked Emerald out the door. You know, Lucien, you are too softhearted to resort to such measures."

"I was once," I confessed, "but I think under Polydore régime I am getting stoical enough to follow in Huldah's footsteps and go her one better."

Our conversation was interrupted by the entrance of Diogenes.

Silvia screamed.

Turning to see what the latest Polydore perpetration might be, I saw that Diogenes was frothing at the mouth.

"Oh, he's having a fit!" exclaimed Silvia frantically. "Call Huldah! Put him in a hot bath. Quick, Lucien, turn on the hot water."

"Not I," I refused grimly. "Let him have a fit and fall in it."

"He ain't got no fit," was the cheerful assurance of Pythagoras, as he sauntered in.

"Your mother would have one," I told him, "if she could hear your English."

"What is the matter with him?" asked Silvia. "Does he often foam in this way?"

"He's been eating your tooth powder," explained Pythagoras. "He likes it 'cause it tastes like peppermint, and then he drank some water before he swallowed the powder and it all fizzed up and run out his mouth."

"I wondered," said Silvia ruefully, "what made my tooth powder disappear so rapidly. What shall I do!"

"Resort to strategy!" I advised. "Lock up your powder hereafter and fill an empty bottle with powdered alum or something worse and leave it around handy."

"Lucien!" exclaimed my wife, who could not seem to recover from this latest annoyance, "I don't see how you can be so fond of children. I did hope—for your sake and on account of Uncle Issachar's offer—that I'd like to have one, but I'd rather go to the poorhouse! I'd almost lose your affection rather than have a child."

"But, Silvia!" I remonstrated in dismay, "you shouldn't judge all by these. They're not fair samples. They're not children—not home-grown children."

"I should say not!" agreed Huldah, who had come into the room. "They are imps—imps of the devil."

I believe she was right. They had a generally demoralizing effect on our household. I was growing irritable, Silvia careworn. Even Huldah showed their influence by acquiring the very latest in slang from them. Once in a while to my amusement I heard Silvia unconsciously adopting the Polydore argot.

As the result of their better nourishment at our table, the imps of the devil daily grew more obstreperous and life became so burdensome to Silvia that I proposed moving away to a childless neighborhood.

"They'd find us out," said Silvia wearily, "wherever we went. Distance would be no obstacle to them."

"Then we might move out of town, as a last resort," I suggested. "Rob says he thinks there is a good legal field in—"

"No, Lucien," vetoed Silvia. "You've a fine practice here, and then there's that attorneyship for the Bartwell Manufacturing Company."

My hope of securing this appointment meant a good deal to us. We were now living up to every cent of my income and though we had the necessities, it was the luxuries of life I craved—for Silvia's sake. She was a lover of music and we had no piano. She yearned to ride and she had no horse. We both had longings for a touring-car and we wanted to travel.

"I've thought of a scheme for a little respite from the sight and sound of the Polydores," I remarked one day. "We'll enter them in the public school. There are four more weeks yet before the long summer vacation."

"That would be too good to be true," declared Silvia. "Five or six hours each day, and then, too, their deportment will be so dreadful that they will have to stay after school hours."

I thought more likely their deportment would lead to suspension, but forbore to wet-blanket Silvia's hopes.

I made my second call upon the male head of the House of Polydore to recommend and urge that its young scions be sent to the public school. I had misgivings as to the outcome of my proposition, as the Polydore parents believed themselves to be the only fount of learning in the town. To my surprise and intense gratification, my suggestion met with no objections whatever. Felix

Polydore referred me to his wife and said he would abide
by her decision. I found her, of course, buried in books,
but remembering Ptolemy's mode of gaining attention, I
peremptorily closed the volume she was studying.

My audacity attained its object and I proffered my
request, laying great stress on the quietude she would
gain thereby. She replied that attendance at school would
doubtless do them no harm, although she expressed her
belief that the most thorough educations were those
obtained outside of schools.

Silvia was wafted into the eighth heaven of bliss and
then some, as the result of my diplomatic mission. Of
course the task of preparing pupils out of the pestiferous
Polydores devolved upon her, but she was actively aided
by the eager and willing Huldah and between them they
pushed the project that promised such an elysium with all
speed. The prospective pupils themselves were not wildly
enthusiastic over this curtailment of their liberty, but
Huldah won the day by proposing that they carry their
luncheon with them, promising an abundant supply of
sugared doughnuts and small pies.

Pythagoras foresaw recreation ahead in the opportunity
to "lick all the kids," and I assumed that Ptolemy had deep
laid schemes for the outmaneuvering of teachers, but as
his left hand never made confidant of his right, I could not
expect to fathom the workings of his mind.

Early on a Monday morning, therefore, our household
arose to lick our Polydore protégés into a shape presentable
for admission to school. It took two hours to pull up
stockings and make them stay pulled, tie shoestrings, comb

out tangles, adjust collars and neckties, to say nothing of vigorous scrubbings to five grimy faces and ten dirt-stained hands.

At last with an air of achievement Silvia corralled her round-up and unloaded the four eldest upon the public school and then proceeded to install the protesting Diogenes in a nursery kindergarten. Huldah stood in the doorway as they marched off and sped the parting guests with a muttered "Good riddance to bad rubbish."

Silvia returned radiant, but her rejoicing was shortlived. She had scarcely taken off her hat and gloves when the four oldest came trooping and whooping into the house.

"What's the matter?" gasped Silvia.

"Got to be vaccinated," explained Ptolemy with an appreciative grin. Of all the Polydores he was the one who had least objected to scholastic pursuits, but he seemed quite jubilant at our discomfiture.

We were somewhat reluctant to undertake the responsibility of their inoculation, especially after Ptolemy told us that his mother didn't believe in vaccination.

"I'll take 'em down and get 'em vaccinated right," declared Huldah. "Their ma won't never notice the scars, and if one of you young uns blabs about it," she added, turning upon them ferociously, "I'll cut your tongue out."

"Suppose there should be some ill result from it," said Silvia apprehensively.

"Don't you worry!" exclaimed Huldah. "Most likely it won't amount to anything. It'll take some new kind of scabs to work in these brats. They're too tough to take anything.

Come on now with me," she commanded, "and after it's done, I'll get you each an ice cream sody."

Through Huldah's efficiency the vaccination was quickly accomplished and the children of our neighbor were reluctantly accepted by the school authorities.

The Polydores were not parted by reason of dissimilarity of age or learning, as they were put into the ungraded room. To keep them there enrolled taxed to the utmost our ingenuity in the way of framing excuses for their repeated cases of tardiness and suspension.

Silvia felt a little remorseful when she listened to the tale of woe recited to her by their teacher at a card party one Saturday afternoon.

"She said," my wife repeated, "that yesterday Pythagoras brought two mice to school in his marble-bag and let them loose. She doesn't believe in corporal punishment, but she determined to experiment with its effect on Pythagoras, so she kept him and Emerald, who was slightly implicated, after school and sent the latter out to get a whip. When he came back he said: 'I couldn't find any stick, but here's some rocks you can throw at him,' and handed her a hat full of stones. This made her too hysterical to try her experiment, so she took away his recess for a week."

"We ought to make her a present," I observed.

"She said," continued Silvia, "that they had given her nervous prostration, but she had no time to prostrate, and if she didn't succeed in getting them graded by the coming fall term, she should accept an offer of marriage she had received from a cross-eyed man, and you know how unlucky that would be, Lucien!"

"We may be driven to worse things than that by fall," I replied ruefully.

# IV

# In Which We Take Boarders

Four weeks of unalloyed bliss and then the summer
vacation times arrived, bringing joy to the heart of the
Polydores and the teacher of the ungraded room, but deep
gloom to the hearthside of the Wades.

One misfortune always brings another. A rival
applicant received the coveted attorneyship and we bade a
sad farewell to piano, saddle-horse, automobile and journey,
the furnishings to our Little House of Dreams.

"I did want you to have a car, Lucien," sighed Silvia,
regretfully, "and you worked so hard this last year, you need
a trip. Won't you go somewhere with Rob—without me?"

I assured her it would be no vacation without her.

"Do you know, Lucien," she proposed diffidently, "I
think it would be an excellent plan to invite Uncle Issachar
to visit us. He knows no more about children than I do—

than I did, I mean, and if he should see the Polydores he'd give us five thousand each for the children we didn't have."

I wouldn't consent to this plan. I had met Uncle Issachar once. He was a crusty old bachelor with a morbid suspicion that everyone was working him for his money. I don't wonder he thought so. He had no other attractions.

Perceiving the strength of my opposition Silvia sweetly and sagaciously refrained from further pressure.

"We should not repine," she said. "We have health and happiness and love. What are pianos and cars and trips compared to such assets?"

What, indeed! I admitted that things might be worse.

Alas! All too soon was my statement substantiated. That night after we had gone to bed, I heard a taxicab sputtering away at the house next door.

"The Polydores must have unexpected guests," I remarked.

"I trust they brought no children with them," murmured Silvia drowsily.

The next morning while we were at breakfast, the odor of June roses wafting in through the open window, the delicious flavor of red-ripe strawberries tickling our palate, and the anticipation of rice griddle-cakes exhilarating us, the millennium came.

For the five young Polydores bore down upon us *en masse.*

"Father and mother have gone away," proclaimed Ptolemy, who was always spokesman for the quintette.

This intelligence was of no particular interest to us—not then, at least. We rarely saw father and mother

Polydore, and they were apparently of no need to their offspring.

Ptolemy's next announcement, however, was startling and effective in its dramatic intensity.

"We've come over to stay with you while they are away."

I laughed; jocosely, I thought.

Silvia paid no heed to my forced hilarity, but ejaculated gaspingly:

"Why, what do you mean!"

"They have gone away somewhere," enlightened our oracle. "They went to the train last night in a taxi. They have gone somewhere to find out something about some kind of aborigines."

"Which reminds me," I remarked reminiscently, "of the man who traveled far and vainly in search of a certain plant which, on his return, he found growing beside his own doorstep."

Silvia paid no heed to my misplaced pleasantry. She was right—as usual. It was no time for levity.

"I don't see," spoke my unappreciative wife, addressing Ptolemy, "why their absence should make any difference in your remaining at home. Gladys can cook your meals and put Diogenes to bed as usual."

"Gladys has gone," piped Demetrius. "She left yesterday afternoon. She was only staying till she could get her pay."

"Father forgot to get another girl in her place," informed Ptolemy, "and he forgot to tell mother he had forgotten until just before they went to the train. She said it didn't matter—that we could just as well come over here and stay with you."

"She said," added Pythagoras, "that you were so crazy over children, that probably you'd be glad to have us stay with you all the time."

My last strawberry remained poised in mid-air. It was quite apparent to me now that there was nothing funny about this situation.

"Milk, milk!" whimpered Diogenes, pulling at Silvia's dress and making frantic efforts to reach the cream pitcher.

Huldah had come in with the griddle-cakes during this avalanche of news.

"Here, all you kids!" commanded our field marshal, as she picked up Diogenes, "beat it to the kitchen, and I'll give you some breakfast. Hustle up!"

The Polydores, whose eyes were bulging with expectancy and semi-starvation, tumbled over each other in their eagerness to "hustle up and beat it to the kitchen." Our oiler of troubled waters followed, and there was assurance of a brief lull.

"What shall we do!" I exclaimed helplessly when the door had closed on the last Polydore. I felt too limp and impotent to cope with the situation. Not so Silvia.

"Do!" she echoed with an intensity of tone and feeling I had never known her to display. "Do! We'll do something, I am sure! I will not for a moment submit to such an imposition. Who ever heard of such colossal nerve! That father and mother should be brought back and prosecuted. I shall report them to the Society for the Prevention of

Cruelty to Children. But we won't wait for such procedure. We'll express each and every Polydore to them at once."

"I should certainly do that P.D.Q. and C.O.D.," I acquiesced, "if the Polydore parents could be located, but you know the abodes of aborigines are many and scattered."

My remarks seemed to fall as flat as the flapjacks I was siruping.

Silvia arose, determination in every lineament and muscle, and crossed the room. She opened the door leading into the kitchen.

"Ptolemy," she demanded, "where have your father and mother gone?"

He came forward and replied in a voice somewhat smothered by cakes and sirup.

"I don't know. They didn't say."

"We can find out from the ticket-agent," I optimistically assured her.

"They never bother to buy tickets. Pay on the train," Ptolemy explained.

My legal habit of counter-argument asserted itself.

"We can easily ascertain to what point their baggage was checked," I remarked, again essaying to maintain a rôle of good cheer.

But the pessimistic Ptolemy was right there with another of his gloom-casting retaliations.

"They only took suit-cases and they always keep them in the car. Here's a check father said to give you to pay for our board. He said you could write in any amount you wanted to."

"He got a lot of dough yesterday," informed Pythagoras, "and he put half of it in the bank here."

Ptolemy handed over a check which was blank except for Felix Polydore's signature.

"I don't see," I weakly exclaimed when my wife had closed the kitchen door, "why she put them off on *us*. Why didn't she trade her brats off for antiques?"

Silvia eyed the check wistfully. I could read the unspoken thought that here, perhaps, was the opportunity for our much-desired trip.

"No, Silvia," I answered quickly, "not for any number of blank checks or vacation trips shall you have the care and annoyance of those wild Comanches."

"I know what I'll do!" she exclaimed suddenly. "I'll go right down to the intelligence office and get anything in the shape of a maid and put her in charge of the Polydore caravansary with double wages and every night out and any other privileges she requests."

This seemed a sane and sensible arrangement, and I wended my way to my office feeling that we were out of the woods.

When I returned home at noon, I found that we had only exchanged the woods for water—and deep water at that.

I beheld a strange sight. Silvia sat by our bedroom window twittering soft, cooing nonsensical nothings to Diogenes, who was clasped in her arms, his flushed little face pressed close to her shoulder.

"He's been quite ill, Lucien. I was frightened and called the doctor. He said it was only the slight fever that children are subject to. He thought with good care that he'd be all right in a few days."

"Did you succeed in getting a cook to go to the Polydores?" I asked anxiously. "You'll need a nurse to go there, too, to take care of Diogenes."

She looked at me reproachfully and rebukingly.

"Why, Lucien! You don't suppose I could send this sick baby back to that uninviting house with only hired help in charge! Besides, I don't believe he'd stay with a stranger. He seems to have taken a fancy to me."

Diogenes confirmed this belief by a languid lifting of his eyelids, as he feelingly patted her cheek with his baby fingers.

I forebore to suggest that the fancy seemed to be mutual. Diogenes, sick, was no longer an "imp of the devil," but a normal, appealing little child. It occurred to me that possibly the care of a sick Polydore might develop Silvia's tiny germ of children.

"Keep him here of course," I agreed, "but—the other children must return home."

"Diogenes would miss them," she said quickly, "and the doctor says his whims must be humored while he is sick. He is almost asleep now. I think he will let me put him down in his own little bed. Ptolemy brought it over here. Pull back the covers for me, Lucien. There!"

Diogenes half opened his eyes, as she laid him in the bed and smiled wanly.

"Mudder!" he cooed.

Silvia flushed and looked as if she dreaded some expression of mirth from me. Relieved by my silence and a suggestion of moisture in the region of my eyes—the day was quite warm—she confessed:

"He has called me that all the morning."

"It would be a wise Polydore that knows its own parents," I observed.

The slight illness of Diogenes lasted three or four days. I still shudder to recall the memory of that hideous period. Silvia's time and attention were devoted to the sick child. Huldah was putting in all her leisure moments at the dentist's, where she was acquiring her third set of teeth, and joy rode unconfined and unrestrained with our "boarders."

Polydore proclivities made the Reign of Terror formerly known as the French Revolution seem like an ice-cream festival. I don't regard myself as a particularly nervous man, but there's a limit! Their war whoops and screeches got on my nerves and temper to the extent of sending me into their midst one evening brandishing a whip and commanding immediate silence. I got it. Not through fear of chastisement, for fear was an emotion unknown to a Polydore, but from astonishment at so unexpected a procedure from so unexpected a source. Heretofore I had either ignored them or frolicked with them. Before they had recovered from their shock, Silvia appeared on the scene.

"Diogenes," she informed them, "was not used to such unwonted quiet, and was fretting at the unaccustomed stillness. Would the boys please play Indian or some of their games again?"

The boys would. I backed from the room, the whip behind me, carefully kept without Silvia's angle of vision.

Before Ptolemy resumed his rôle of chief, he bestowed a
knowing and maddening wink upon me.

I wished that we had remained neighborless. I wished
that the aborigines would scalp Felix Polydore and the
writer of Modern Antiquities. Then we could land their
brats on the Probate Court. I wished that this were the reign
of Herod. I vowed I would backslide from the Presbyterian
faith since it no longer included in its articles of belief
the eternal damnation of infants. How long, O Catiline,
would—

A paralyzing suspicion flashed into the maelstrom of
my vituperative maledictions. I rushed wildly upstairs to
our combination bedroom, sickroom, and nursery, where
Silvia sat like a guardian angel beside the Polydore patient.

"Silvia," I shouted excitedly, "do you suppose those
diabolical Polydore parents purposely played this trick on
us? Was it a premeditated Polydore plan to abandon their
young? And can you blame them for playing us for easy
marks? Could any parents, Polydore, or otherwise, ever
come back to such fiends as these?"

"Hush!" she cautioned, without so much as a glance in
my direction. "You'll wake Diogenes!"

Wake Diogenes! Ye Gods! And she had also implored
the brothers of Diogenes to continue their anvil chorus!
This took the last stitch of starch from my manly bosom.
Spiritless and spineless I bore all things, believed all
things—but hoped for nothing.

# V

# In Which We Take a Vacation

Diogenes finally convalesced to his former state
of ruggedness and obstreperousness. He continued,
however, to cling to Silvia and to call her "mudder." To my
amusement the other children followed suit and she was
now "muddered" by all the Polydores.

"I am glad," I remarked, "that they scorn to include
me in their adoption. I wouldn't fancy being 'faddered' by
the Polydores."

"You won't be," Ptolemy, appearing seemingly from
nowhere, assured me. "We've named you stepdaddy."

"If it be possible, Silvia," I implored, "let this cup pass
from me."

"I am going down to the intelligence office today,"
replied Silvia soothingly. "Diogenes is well enough to go

home now, and I can run over there every evening and see that he is properly put to bed."

I went down town feeling like a mule relieved of his pack.

When I came home that afternoon, I found Silvia sitting on the shaded porch serenely sewing. A Sabbath-like stillness pervaded. Not a Polydore in sight or sound.

"Oh!" I cried buoyantly. "The Polydores have been returned to their home station!"

"No," she replied calmly. "They told me at the intelligence office that it would be absolutely impossible to persuade, bribe, or hire a servant to assume the charge of the Polydore place."

"I suppose," I said glumly, "that Gladys gave the job a double cross. But will you please account for the phenomenon of the utter absence of Polydores at the present period? Has Huldah at last carried out her oft-repeated threat of exterminating the Polydore race?"

"Pythagoras," explained Silvia dejectedly, "has gone to the doctor's. He broke his wrist this morning. Diogenes is lost and Emerald has gone to look for him—"

"Oh, why hunt him up?" I remonstrated. "Maybe Emerald, too, will get lost or strayed or stolen."

"Huldah," continued Silvia, "has locked Demetrius in the cellar. I am unable to report on Ptolemy. Huldah is half sick, but she won't go to bed. She said no beds in Bedlamite for her. But I have a wonderful plan to suggest. There is relief in sight if you will consent."

"I will consent to any committable crime on the calendar," I assured her, "that will lead to the parting of the Polydore path from ours. Divulge."

"We both need a change and rest. Today I heard of a most alluring, inexpensive, unfrequented resort called Hope Haven. Unfashionable, fine fishing, beautiful scenery, twelve miles from a railroad, and a stage stops there but once a day."

"If there is such a place, we'll go there at once, though why such an enticing spot should be unfrequented is beyond me. Do we leave the Polydores to their fate, or as a town charge?"

"We'll leave them to Huldah. She offered to keep them here if we'd take the outing. She said she'd either give them free rein or beat their brains out."

"Then I see where the Polydores land in a juvenile jail, or else I return to defend Huldah for a charge of murder. We'll take our departure by night—tomorrow night—and like the Arabs, or the Polydore parents, silently steal away."

"Lucien," said Silvia constrainedly, when we had arranged the details of our plan, "if you wouldn't object too much, I should like to take Diogenes with us. He hasn't missed his mother, but I really believe he'd be homesick without me."

"Take him, of course," I said. "He's manageable away from the others. I plainly see you've formed the Polydore habit, and maybe a partial parting from the Polydores would be wiser, but we'll take Diogenes as an antidote against too perfect a time. But I forgot to tell you that I had a letter from Rob today. He plans to come and make his visit now and will arrive next Monday. I'll write him to join us at Hope Haven. You must write down again for me the route we take to get there."

Silvia laughed hopelessly.

"It never rains but it pours. I had a letter from Beth this afternoon, and she says she would like to come to us now. She arrives Monday. Here is her letter."

"Great minds! It is quite a coincidence," I declared.

"I thought it would be so nice to have Beth go with us to this resort."

"It can't be done," I said. "That is, they can't both go. I am not going to let even Rob Rossiter slight my sister."

"Still it would be a triumph to have her change his mind—or his heart. You know a woman-hater always succumbs to the right girl."

"In books, yes!"

I had been scanning Beth's letter and I laughed derisively as I read aloud: "'I am so curious to see those next-door children. When you first wrote of the "Polydores" I never once thought of them as children.'"

"She thought exactly right," I told Silvia, and then continued reading: "'I supposed them to be something like tadpoles or polliwogs. I really think I shall enjoy them.'"

"It would serve her right," I said, "to let her come and stay with them here in our absence. She'd get the cure for enjoyment all right. Rob wrote of them in the same strain and says he, too, is curious to meet the missing links."

"Does she know," asked Silvia, "how Rob regards women?"

"No; I've always made some excuse to her for not having them meet. I didn't want to hear her make disparaging remarks about him, and she is such a flirt, she'd try to draw him out and he would shut up like a clam."

"Well, I think," decided Silvia, "that the best way out of it is to write Rob to postpone his visit and I will write Beth to come direct to Hope Haven."

"Yes," I agreed, "that will be fine. She shall have charge of dear little Di and study the evolutions of the Polydores later."

I approved this plan. So we wrote our letters and stealthily, but joyously, prepared for our getaway, leaving the house like thieves in the night and bearing the sleeping cherub, Diogenes.

Silvia sighed in relief when we were aboard the train.

"I feel quite chesty," she declared, "at being smart enough to outwit Ptolemy, the wizard."

"I have the feeling," I observed forebodingly, "that they may be on the train or underneath it."

The next morning we reached Windy Creek, the station nearest our destination, and continued our journey by stage.

"People will think you have consoled yourself very speedily for the death of your first husband," I observed, as we were en route.

"Why, what do you mean, Lucien?"

"You know Diogenes addresses me as stepdaddy. It is the only word he speaks plainly."

"Oh!" she exclaimed in perturbation, "I never thought of that! Well, we can explain to everyone, or I'll teach them to leave off the 'step.'"

"Not on your life!" I demurred.

"He had better call you Lucien, then. Emerald calls his father 'Felix.'"

She at once began her tutelage of the bewildered Diogenes. After several stabs at pronouncing Lucien he managed to evolve "Ocean" to which he sometimes affixed "step" so that people to whom he was not explained doubtless thought me the latest thing in dances.

Hope Haven was like most resorts—a place safe to shun. There was a low, flat stretch of woods in which a clearing had been made for a barn-like structure called a hotel, with rooms rough and not always ready. The beautiful recreation grounds mentioned in the advertising matter consisted of a plowed field worked over into a space designated as a tennis court and a grass-grown croquet ground.

"Anyway," claimed Silvia hopefully, "it's a treat to see woods, water, and sky unconfined."

She devoted the remainder of the morning to unpacking and after luncheon set off to explore the woods, borrowing from the landlady a little cart for Diogenes to ride in. My plan to go in swimming was delayed by my garrulous landlord.

I was just starting for the lake when I heard sounds from the woods that alarmed the landlord but which I instantly recognized as the Polydore yell. A moment later I saw Silvia emerging at full speed into the open, drawing the cart in which Diogenes was doubled up like a jackknife. I hastened to meet them.

"Oh, Lucien," exclaimed my wife tearfully, "we are bitten to bits! Just look at poor little Di!"

I lifted the howling child from the cart. His face, neck, and hands were stringy and purplish—a cross between an eggplant and a round steak.

"Mosquitoes!" explained Silvia. "They came in flocks and they advertised particularly 'no mosquitoes.'"

A dour-faced guest paused in passing.

"There aren't—many," she declared. "Very few, in fact, compared to the number of black flies, sand fleas, and jiggers. However, you'll find more discomfort from the poison ivy, I imagine."

"Lucien," began Silvia in lament.

"Never mind!" I hastened to console, "you are out of the woods now, and you won't have to go in again. I presume they have an antidote up at the house. I'll give you and Diogenes first aid and then we will all go down to the lake shore. You can both sit on the dock and watch me swim."

They both brightened up, and when we reached the hotel the landlady provided a soothing lotion for the bites and stings. By the time we had started for the lake, the afflicted two were in holiday spirit again.

I sought cover in a small shed called a bath-house and got into my swimming outfit and shot out from the dipping end of the diving-board into the water. When I came to the surface, Silvia, sitting beside Diogenes on the dock, shrieked wildly.

"Oh, Lucien, there are snakes all around you! Come out, quick!"

"They are only water snakes," I assured her.

"I don't care what kind they are. They are snakes just the same."

Diogenes instantly began to bellow for me to hand him a snake to play with.

"He recognizes his own," I told Silvia, who, however, saw nothing amusing in my implication.

When I came out of the water, the temperature had climbed several degrees and we were glad to seek the hotel parlor, which was cool and damp.

After dinner Silvia put Diogenes to bed and we sat out on the veranda. I was enjoying my evening smoke and the feel of the night wind in my face. Silvia had just finished telling me that merely to be away from the Polydores was Paradise enough for her, and that she didn't care very much about the woods, anyway—the lake was sufficient, when her optimism was rudely jolted by the shrill, shudder-sending song of the festive mosquito.

She fled into the parlor. The landlady, who seemed to have a panacea for all ills, suggested that she might tack mosquito netting around the little balcony extending from our bedroom, and then she could sit there in comfort when the mosquitoes bothered.

"That's what the last lady that had that room did," she said, "but when she left, she took the netting with her. We keep a supply in our little store."

Silvia immediately sought the hotel store and bought a quantity of the netting and a goodly stock of the mosquito lotion.

That night as I was drifting into slumber, Silvia remarked: "Only one of the things I heard and read about this place is true."

"Which one?" I asked between winks.

"That it was unfrequented. I have seen only three guests besides us so far. How do they make it pay?"

"The hotel is evidently only a side issue," I replied.

"To what?"

"To the store. Think of the quantities of lotion and netting they must sell in the season, which, you must know, is in the fall. The hunting, the landlord tells me, is very good, and his hotel is quite popular in October and November."

"I think we had better stay, Lucien. Mosquitoes don't poison you."

"Even if they did," I declared, "as a choice between them and the Polydores I would say, 'Oh, Mosquito, where is thy sting?'"

# VI

# A Flirt and a Woman-Hater

The next morning I arose early and screened in the little birdhouse balcony. There was a large piece of netting left and Silvia converted it into a robe and headgear for the swaddling of Diogenes.

"He looks like the Bride of Lammermoor," I declared, as he went forth in this regalia.

"Well, that's preferable to looking like a pest-house patient, as he did yesterday."

His first-aid costume didn't find favor with the landlady, as it would seem indicative to the newly arrived of the features of the place. However, before another stage-coming was due, Di had rent his garment sufficiently to make it useless as a "skeeter skirt."

During the morning I enjoyed my solitary swim with the snakes. Diogenes played football with the croquet balls and bruised one of his toes, besides hitting the landlady's child in the eye. Silvia went for a walk which had been pictured in the advertisements. She speedily returned, her ardor dampened.

"There are so many sticks and stones and rocks," she said in a discouraged tone, "that there was no pleasure in walking. I nearly sprained my ankle."

"Well, the real sport we haven't tried yet," I said. "We'll get a boat and take Diogenes and go for a row on the lake."

This proposition met with instant favor. I put Silvia and Diogenes in the stern of the boat and pulled for the opposite shore. My endeavors to gain this point were balked by Silvia's remarkable conceptions of the art of steering craft. She was so serenely satisfied, however, with the way she performed her duties and the aid she thought she was giving me, that I forbore to criticize.

In order to achieve a few strokes in the right direction, I asked her to get me a cigar from an inside pocket of my coat, which was on the seat in front of her. Then came the blight to our bliss. She looked in the wrong pocket and instead of producing a cigar, she extracted two letters with seals unbroken.

"Lucien Wade!" she gasped. "Here are our letters to Beth and Rob. Well, it is my fault. I should have known better than to give them to you."

"The plot thickens," I replied thoughtfully.

"This is Monday. They must both be at the house now. What will they think!"

"They will think we didn't receive their letters."

"Isn't it unfortunate—," she began.

"No," I replied. "I am not sure but what it is a good thing. It will give Rob a jolt to see that girls can be as nice as Beth is, and as for her, she is quite able to take care of the situation where a man is concerned."

"But we must have Beth here. Maybe you'd better telegraph her."

"Huldah understands conditions. She will send Beth on here."

The next morning we took Diogenes and went down the road to meet the stage. As it came around the curve, we saw there were three passengers.

"Tolly!" cried Diogenes with an ecstatic whoop.

"Beth!" recognized Silvia.

"Rob!" I ejaculated.

The stage stopped to allow us to get in.

Mutual explanations followed. Ours were brief and substantiated by the documents in evidence.

"Now," I said turning threateningly to Ptolemy, "what did you come here for?"

"To show them," indicating Beth and Rob, "how to get here and to look after Di so you and mudder could enjoy your vacation," he replied glibly.

Beth laughed mirthfully.

"Check! Lucien."

"Didn't Huldah warn you," I asked her, "that our whereabouts were to remain unknown?"

"Ptolemy," she replied, "is evidently a mind reader, for he told me where you were before I saw Huldah."

"Why, Ptolemy, how did you know where we were?" asked Silvia.

"I was on top of the porch when you told stepdaddy about coming. I didn't tell the others. I won't bother you any. And I know how to look after Di. You won't send me back, mudder," he pleaded, looking wistfully at the foam-crested water of the little lake.

I wondered mutely if Silvia could resist the appeal in the eyes of the neglected boy when he turned his imploring gaze to hers, and the delight depicted in Diogenes' eyes at "Tolly's" arrival. She could not.

"You may stay as long as we do," she said slowly, "if you are a good boy and will not play too rough with Diogenes."

We had reached the hotel by this time, and with a wild "ki yi" Ptolemy dashed for the shore, dragging the delighted Diogenes with him.

"It's only fair to Huldah to take one more off her hands," Silvia said apologetically.

"Them Three is what bothers me," I complained. "If they, too, follow after, Heaven help them! I won't."

"It's a good arrangement all around," declared Rob. "I judge it takes a Polydore to understand his ilk, so the kids can pair off together. Miss Wade will be company for you, while Lucien and I go fishing."

He looked keenly at Beth as he spoke, but Beth was looking demurely down and made no sign of having heard him.

Silvia and I went with Beth to her room, and then she told her story.

"Knowing Lucien's failing, I was not surprised at receiving no response to my letter. When I got out of the cab in front of your house, a wild-looking boy, very bas-relief as to eyes, and who I felt sure must be Ptolemy of the Polydores, appeared. As soon as he saw me he gave utterance to a blood-curdling yell of—'Here she is!'

"In response to his call three of his understudies came on with headlong greeting.

"'You are Beth, aren't you?' Ptolemy asked me. Then he drew me aside and in mysterious whispers told me where you were and that you had written me to join you here. He added that stepdaddy never remembered to mail letters. I went within and interviewed Huldah who confirmed his information.

"Presently I saw a taxi stop before the house.

"'That's him!' exclaimed Ptolemy.

"'Him who?' I asked.

"'Rob somebody—stepdaddy's college chum. He wrote he was coming, and they thought they had postponed him.'

"With a sprint of speed the four Polydores surrounded your Mr. Rossiter, all talking at once. I came to the rescue, of course, and explained the situation, and we decided to follow you.

"Ptolemy was promoter for the trip and suggested the advisability of his accompanying us as courier and future nursemaid to Diogenes. He was intending to come anyway, but thought he'd wait for us. He had all his belongings packed."

"He hasn't many except those he had on," said Silvia thoughtfully.

"He has some swimming trunks, two collars, two shirts, some mismated socks, homemade fishing tackle and a battered baseball bat. We came away surreptitiously to escape detection by the trio left behind. I knew you wouldn't welcome his presence—but he said he was coming anyway, so we thought we might as well bring him and express him back."

After visiting with Beth for a few moments, Silvia and I withdrew to talk matters over confidentially.

"All's well that ends well," I quoth.

"It hasn't ended yet," reminded Silvia. "I trust Ptolemy didn't reveal what you said about Rob's being a woman-hater and Beth a flirt."

Ptolemy conveniently appeared just then, as he generally did in the midst of private interviews. Silvia asked him if he had repeated those remarks to Beth or Rob.

"Why, no," he said. "I knew you didn't want her to know, because stepdaddy said so, and I thought he wouldn't like to be called that, and I wasn't going to give Beth away to him."

"You're all right, Ptolemy!" I exclaimed, for the first time awarding him approbation.

Out on the veranda we met Rob.

"Say, those Polydores certainly have the punch and pep," he declared. "I'd like to have fetched the whole bunch along with me."

"If you had," I replied dryly, "our life's friendship would have died on the spot."

# VII

## In Which Nothing
## Much Happens

"Why Hope Haven?" asked Rob reflectively, when he had taken inventory of the possibilities of the resort.

"Because," sighed Silvia, "so many hopes—vacation hopes—must have been buried here."

Rob was of an investigating turn of mind, however, and he had heard from a native of H. H., as he had abbreviated the place, that there was a smaller lake, abounding in fish, farther on through the forest. It was so strongly fortified, however, by the formidable battalions of sharp-shooting insects that but few fishermen had ever been able to lay siege to it.

Rob and I being poison proof decided to try our luck and pitch camp for a few days on the shores of this hidden treasure. As we had to send to town by the stage driver for the necessary supplies, we remained in H. H. the remainder of the day.

We at once paired off in Noah's most approved style as Rob had outlined. Beth and Ptolemy went up shore, sticks and stones and rocks being no obstacles to their feet. Rob and I sought the society of the snakes, while Silvia and Diogenes, mosquito-netted, watched a game of croquet.

We dined without the pleasure of the society of Ptolemy and Diogenes, who had been invited to sit at the table with the landlady's children. I might state, incidentally, that the invitation was never repeated.

Beth was quite excited over her walk.

"Ptolemy and I," she boasted, "made more of a discovery than Mr. Rossiter did. We found a haunted house, a perfectly haunted house."

"I am not surprised," declared Silvia. "You couldn't expect any other kind of a house in such a region."

"Where is it?" I asked, "and what is it haunted by?"

"Insects," suggested Silvia.

"You go around shore about two miles, only it's farther, as you have to make so many ups and downs over the rocks. Then you leave the shore and go through a low marshy stretch, sort of a Dismal Swamp, and then up a hill. After Ptolemy and I climbed to the top, we looked down and saw, hidden in a clump of lonely-looking poplars, a small, rudely built house. We went down to explore and had hard work making our way through a thick growth of—everything. We crawled under some tangled vines and came up on the steps. The house was vacant, although there were a few old pieces of furniture—a couple of cots, a cook-stove, table, and chairs.

"On our way home we met a woman who gave us a history of the house. An old miser lived there long ago. One night he was robbed and murdered, and his ghost still haunts the place. No one ventures in its vicinity, and she said most likely we were the first people who had gone there since the tragedy. She told us of a nearer way to reach it. You take the road to Windy Creek, and about two miles below here, turn into a lane and then go through a grove and over a hill."

"You don't really believe the story, that is, the ghost part of it?" asked Rossiter.

"N—o," allowed Beth. "Still, I'd like to. It makes it interesting. Ptolemy and I are going down there some night to see if we can find the ghost."

"You won't see one," I assured her. "Ptolemy's presence would be sufficient to keep even a ghost in the background."

"Ptolemy's a peach," declared Beth emphatically.

"If he were older, you wouldn't think so," said Rob.

"Why not?" asked Beth in surprise, or seeming surprise.

He smiled enigmatically, and irrelevantly asked her if she wouldn't really be afraid to go to the haunted house at night with only Ptolemy for protection.

She assured him she shouldn't be afraid of a ghost if she saw one, and that she shouldn't be afraid to go alone.

Throughout the evening, which we spent in rowing, walking, and later at a little impromptu supper, I was interested in observing the puzzling behavior of Beth and my chum. I had expected that he would avoid her as much as possible and speak to her only when common politeness made conversation obligatory, and that she, a born coquette, would seek to add his scalp to her collection. Instead, to my surprise, their rôles were reversed. He appeared interested in her every remark and looked at her often and intently. He was quite assiduous in his attentions which, strange to say, she discouraged, not with the deep design of a flirt to increase his ardor, but with a calm firmness that admitted of no doubt as to her feelings.

"Your sister," he remarked to me as we were walking down to the lake for a swim just before going to bed, "is a very unusual type."

"Not at all!" I assured him. "Beth is the true feminine type which you have never taken the trouble to know."

"Oh, come, Lucien! Not feminine, you know. Though she is inconsistent."

I resented the imputation hotly, but he only laughed and said that he guessed it was true that a man didn't understand the women in his family as well as an outsider did.

"You think," I said, "just because she says she isn't afraid of ghosts—"

"Not at all," he denied. "That wasn't the reason, but—I like her type, though I always supposed I wouldn't. It is a new one to me—anyway. I didn't think so young a girl as she—"

Our discussion was cut short by the inevitable, ever-present Ptolemy, who came running up to us, clad in about four inches of swimming trunks.

"Why aren't you in bed?" I demanded.

"I was in bed, but it was so warm I couldn't sleep, and I went to the window and saw you coming down here, so I thought I'd come, too."

I repeated Rob's remarks to Silvia when I returned to our room, and she betrayed Beth's confidences in regard to Rob.

"She says she would like him if it were not for one trait that she dislikes more than any other in a man and that it was sufficient in her estimation to counterbalance all his good qualities."

"What can she mean?" I asked bewildered. "I don't see a flaw in Rob, except for his being a woman-hater, and he surely hasn't betrayed that fact to her, judging from his manner toward her. I think he is making an effort to be nice to her on my account, and she doesn't appreciate it."

"I asked her what the flaw was, and she flushed and said she couldn't tell me."

"Well, I guess all around it is a good thing we are going off on our fishing expedition. I don't want my friend turned down by my sister, and I don't want my friend calling my sister a new type and unfeminine."

# VIII

## Ptolemy Disappears

When Rob and I, with our camping outfit, drove off through the woods, Ptolemy's eyes followed us so enviously and he pleaded so eloquently to be taken with us that Rob was actually on the point of considering it.

"See here, Rob Rossiter!" I exclaimed, "This is my vacation and all I came to this God-forsaken place for was to escape the Polydores. If he goes, I stay. You know I've always tried to meet issues, but this antique family has got me going."

"All right," he yielded.

After a drive of a few miles we came to the lake and pitched our tent. Two days of ideal camp life followed. The weather was fine, Rob was a first-class cook, and the sport was beyond our most optimistic expectation. We landed enough of the Friday food to satisfy the most fastidious fishing fiend, and the mosquitoes, finding we were impervious to their stings, finally let us alone.

I forgot all business cares and disappointments, yes, even the Polydores; but on the morning of the third day Rob began to show signs of restlessness and spoke of the likelihood of my wife's being lonely.

"Not with Beth and Ptolemy in calling distance," I told him.

"But they will be off together," he replied, "and your wife will be alone with that *enfant terrible*. I fancy, too, that your sister isn't exactly a companion for your wife."

"Well, that shows how little you know her. She and Silvia are great friends."

"Oh, yes, of course they are friendly, but I mean their tastes are so different, and they are so unlike. Your sister doesn't care for domesticity."

"Sure she does. You have turned the wrong searchlight on Beth. If you knew her, you'd like her."

"I do like her," he declared. "It's too bad she—"

He stopped abruptly and quickly changed the conversation. In spite of my efforts to renew the controversy about Beth, he refused to return to the subject.

In the afternoon, when I was doing a little scale work preparatory to cooking, a messenger from the hotel drove up with a note from Silvia which I read aloud:

"Ptolemy has been missing for twenty-four hours. We are in hopes he has joined you. If not, what shall I do?"

"We'll go back with you," said Rob to the man. "Just lend a hand here and help us pull up these tent stakes."

He pleaded eloquently to be taken with us.

"What's Ptolemy to me or I to him?" I asked with a groan, "can't we give him absent treatment?"

"You're positively inhuman, Lucien," protested Rob. "The boy may be at the bottom of the lake."

"Not he! He was born to be hung."

All this time, however, I had been active in making preparations for departure, as I knew that Silvia would feel that we were responsible for Ptolemy's safety, and her anxiety was reason enough for me to hasten to her.

Rob was quite jubilant on our return trip and declared that the fish came too easily and too plentifully to make it real sport, but I felt that I had another grudge to be charged up to the fateful family.

We found Silvia pale from anxiety, Beth in tears, and Diogenes loudly clamoring for "Tolly." We learned that the afternoon before, Silvia and Beth had gone with the landlady for a ride, leaving Diogenes in Ptolemy's care, but on their return at dinner time, Diogenes was playing alone in the sandpile.

Nothing was thought of Ptolemy's absence until bedtime, and they had then sent out searching parties to the woods and the lake shores. Finally it occurred to Beth that he might have gone to join Rob and me, so they sent the messenger to investigate.

"He must be lost in the woods somewhere," said Beth tearfully, "and he will starve to death."

Rob actually touched her hand in his distress at her grief.

"Ptolemy is too smart to get lost anywhere," I declared. "He knows fully as much about woodcraft as he does about every other kind of craft. He's one of his mother's antiquities personified. But haven't you been able to find anyone who saw him after you went for your ride?"

"No; even the hotel help were all out on the lake."

"And he left Diogenes here, absolutely unguarded?"

"Well!" admitted Silvia, "he tied Diogenes to a tree near the sandpile."

"Then he must have gone away with malice aforethought," I said, "and Diogenes is the only one who knows anything about his last movements."

I lifted the child to my knee, and speaking more gently to him than I had ever done, I asked:

"Di, did you and Tolly play in the sandpile yesterday?"

He was quite emphatic in his affirmative.

"Well, tell Ocean: Did Tolly go away and leave you?"

"Tolly goed away," he confirmed.

"Oh, Lucien!" protested Beth, laughing. "He's too little to know what you are talking about or to remember."

"Lucien's ruling passion strong in death," murmured Rob. "He can't help cross-examining the cradle even!"

"Which way," I resumed, ignoring these interruptions, "did Tolly go—that way?" pointing towards the woods.

"No! Tolly goed—" and he trailed off into his baby jargon which no one could understand, but he pointed to the lake.

"What did he say when he went away; when he tied the rope around you?"

"Bye-bye."

"What else?"

Diogenes' intentions to be communicative were certainly all right, but not a word was intelligible. As he kept picking at his dress and pointing to it, I finally prompted:

"Did Tolly pin a paper to Di's dress?"

"'m—h'—m."

"Bravo, Lucien!" applauded Rob. "They say you can induce a witness to admit anything."

"What did Di do with the paper?" I continued.

The word he wanted evidently being beyond his vocabulary and speech, he made a rotary motion with his fist. The gesture conveyed nothing to our minds, but was instantly recognized and interpreted by the landlady's little girl, who said he meant a windmill such as she had sometimes made for him.

"What did Di do with the windmill?" I asked.

He pointed to the sandpile, which I investigated and found a stick planted therein. I pulled it up and saw a pin sticking in the end of it. Further excavation revealed a crumpled piece of paper on which was written in Ptolemy's round hand:

"Want to see kids. Am going home. Tell Beth I bet she dasent go to the haunted house alone at night. Ptolemy."

"Poor Huldah!" sighed Silvia.

"I thought he was having the time of his life here," said Rob.

"He was sore," declared Beth, "because you and Lucien wouldn't take him with you on the fishing trip. He was moping by himself all the morning."

"Trying to think up some new deviltry," I theorized, "to make us feel bad."

"No," asserted Silvia, "I think he really misses the boys. The Polydores, for all their scrappings, are very clannish. But how do you suppose he got down to Windy Creek?"

"He could catch plenty of rides along the way, but what is puzzling me is how he got the money to pay his fare."

"He seemed very well provided with cash," informed Rob. "I tried to pay for his ticket down here, but he insisted on buying it himself."

Silvia worried so much about what might happen to him en route that after dinner I motored to Windy Creek with some tourists who had stopped at the hotel in passing.

I called up long distance and after some delay got in communication with our house. Ptolemy himself answered and assured me he had arrived all "hunky doory," that Huldah, who was out on an errand, was "hunky doory," and that the kids were all "hunky doory." In fact, his cheerful tone indicated that the whole universe was in the beatific state described by his expressive adjective.

I was really ripping mad at his taking French leave and so giving Silvia cause for her anxiety, but I forbore to reprimand him by word or tone, lest he get even by "coming back" literally. I did tell him how the loss of the note for twenty-four hours had caused a general excitement, but he felt no remorse for his share in the situation, blaming Diogenes entirely and bidding me "punch the kid's face" for unpinning the note.

On my return from Windy Creek I was fortunate enough to fall in with a farmer who lived near the hotel. He was driving some sort of a machine he called an *autoo*. He was an old-timer in the vicinity and related the past, present, and pluperfect of all the residents on the route. I had a detailed and vivid account of the midnight visitor of the haunted house.

"I'd jest naturally like to see what there is to it," he said. "Not that I am afeerd at all, only it's sort of spooky to go to a lonesome place like that all alone. If I could git some one to go with me, I'd tackle the job, but I vum if every time I perpose it to anyone they don't make some excuse."

"I'm on," I declared. "I don't dread ghosts near as much as I do some living folks I know."

"Right you air," chuckled the old man. "If you say so we'll go right off now jest as sure as shootin'. We may be ghosts ourselves tomorrow."

I assured him I was quite ready to encounter the ghost, so he jubilantly turned the machine from the road into a grass-grown lane. We zigzagged for some distance and then got out and went on foot through a grove. The moon and the stars were half veiled by some light, misty clouds, so that the little house didn't show up very clearly, but as we came to the top of the hill, we saw something that shook even my well-behaved nerves.

From a window in the roof-room extended a white arm and hand, with index finger pointing threateningly and directly toward us.

"What's your rush?" I asked, when I had overtaken him.

My farmer friend turned quickly and fled toward the grove. I followed fleetly. "What's your rush?" I asked, when I had overtaken him.

"I just happened to remember," he explained gaspingly, "that there's a pesky autoo thief in these 'ere parts. Bukins had his stole jest last night."

The lights on his machine must have reassured him as to its safety when we emerged from the woods into the open, but he didn't lessen his speed. We got in the "autoo" and soon said good-by to the lane. At one time I believed it was good-by to everything, but at last we gained the highway, right side up.

"Well!" I said, when we were running normally again on terra firma, "that was some little old ghost—beckoned to us to come right in, too!"

"You seen it then!" he exclaimed excitedly. "I'm mighty glad I had an eyewitness. Folks wouldn't believe me."

"They probably won't believe me, either," I assured him. "I am a lawyer."

"You don't tell me! Well, it did jest give me a start for a minute. I'd like to hev gone in and seen it nigh to, if I hadn't happened to think of this 'ere autoo. You see I ain't got it all paid for yet. I'm jest clean beat. You don't mind my takin' a leetle pull at a stone fence, do you?"

"I guess not," I assented somewhat dubiously, however. "That was a rail fence we took a pull at back in the lane, wasn't it? Of course, if we shouldn't happen to clear the stone fence as well as we did the rail fence, it might be more disastrous."

"Oh, land!" he said with a cackling laugh, "I ain't meanin' that kind of a fence. I mean the kind you—Say! You ain't one of them teetotalers, be you?"

"Only in theory," I replied, "but this stone fence drink is a new one on me. What's it like?"

He stopped the "autoo" and pulled a bottle from an inner pocket.

"You kin taste it better than I kin tell it," he declared. "Take a pull—a condumned good one."

I rarely imbibed, confining my indulgences to the demands of necessity, but I thought that the flight of Ptolemy, the ghostly encounter, and my Mazeppa-wild ride all combined to constitute an occasion adequate to call for a bracer in the shape of a stone fence, or anything he might produce.

I took what I considered a "condumned good one" from the bottle and it nearly strangled me, but I followed the aged stranger's advice to take another to "cure the chokes" caused by the first one. On general principles I took a third and then reluctantly returned him the bottle.

"Here's over the moon," he jovially exclaimed as he proceeded to make my attempt at a "condumned good one" appear most niggardly.

"May I ask," I inquired when my feeling of nerve-tense strain had vanished, and I felt as if I were treading thin air, "just what is in a stone fence?"

"Well, what do you think?" he asked slyly.

"I think the very devil is in it," I replied.

"Well, mebby," he admitted. "It's two-thirds hard cider and one-third whisky. It's a healthy, hearting drink and yet it has a leetle come back to it—a sort o' kick, you know. But this is where I live," pointing to a farmhouse well back from the road, "but I am goin' to run you on to your tavern though."

The hotel was dark, save for a light in my room. I invited him in, but he was anxious to "git hum and tell the folks," so I gave him some cigars and went in to "tell my folks."

I found them in the room waiting for me. That is, Beth was in the room, sitting by the table and pretending to read. Silvia and Rob were out in the little balcony. They came inside as soon as they heard my voice.

"Oh, was he there?" asked Silvia anxiously.

"Yes," I replied. "He answered the telephone himself."

I was feeling quite exhilarated by this time. My wife looked a perfect vision to me. Beth, I thought, was some sister, and Rob the best fellow in the world. Even the Polydores at long range, and under the ameliorating influence of stone fences, seemed like fine little fellows— rather active and strenuous, to be sure, but only as all wholesome children should be.

Silvia was relieved at the announcement of Ptolemy's safety, but very much disappointed that I did not succeed in interviewing Huldah and finding out something about domestic affairs.

I assured her that everything was "hunky doory" at home, praised the telephone service, my expedition to town, and painted my return ride with "the honest farmer" in glowing terms. I was suddenly halted in my eulogy by becoming aware of an amazed expression on my wife's countenance, a most suspicious glance in Beth's wide-open eyes, and a very knowing wink from Rob.

"Lucien," said Silvia severely, "I believe you've been drinking. I certainly smell spirits."

"Maybe you do," I replied jocosely. "I certainly saw spirits. I went to the haunted house on my way back."

"I thought Windy Creek was a dry town," remarked Rob innocently.

"It is," I assured him, "but I rode home with an old man—a farmer."

"Does he run a blind pig?" asked Rob.

"It was more like a pig in a poke," I replied.

"Lucien," exclaimed Silvia reproachfully, "you told me two years ago, after that banquet to the Bar, that you were never going to touch wine or whisky again. What did that horrid old man give you?"

"A stone fence. That's what he said it was anyway."

"It's a new one on me," commented Rob.

"There was a new toast went with it. He drank to 'over the moon.'"

"You must have gone there all right and taken all the shine from the moon-man," said Rob.

"Lucien," asked Beth, "did you really go to that haunted house?"

Again I was moved to eloquence, and I told of the farmer's yearning, the fulfillment, the beckoning hand and the beating of the retreat at length.

"Are you sure," asked Rob, "that you didn't take that stone fence before you visited the haunted house?"

"I know," I replied, loftily, "that a lawyer's word is worthless, but seeing is believing. We will all visit the haunted house tomorrow night and I'll make good on ghosts."

This plan was unanimously approved, and then Silvia suggested that she thought I had better go to bed. I had no particular objection to doing so.

"Lucien," she said solemnly, when we were alone, "I want you to promise me something. I want you to give me your word that you will never take another stone wall."

I did this most readily.

# IX

## In Which We See Ghosts

The next morning Rob tried earnestly and vainly to drive a wedge in Beth's good graces, but she treated him with a casual tolerance that finally put him in an ill humor which he took out on me with many a gibe at my "stone fence spirit."

Men of my profession who have to deal with facts rather than fancy are not believers in the supernatural. I was sure that the extending arm and the beckoning finger were there, but belonged to no ghost. It might have been a curtain blowing out the window or a fake of some kind. But I knew that unless there was some kind of a showing in a ghostly way that night, I should never hear the last of my stone fence indulgence, so I resolved to make a preliminary visit alone by daylight and rig up something white to substantiate my spectral narrative.

I didn't find an opportunity to escape unseen until late in the afternoon, when I went, ostensibly, for a solitary row on the lake.

I landed and came by a circuitous route to the haunted house. The calm security of sunshine, of course, prevented any shivers of anticipation such as I had experienced the night before. On passing one of the windows on my way to the front entrance, I glanced in, stopped in sheer fright, stooped and backed to the next window, which was screened by a labyrinth of vines through which I peered. I am sure I lost my Bloom of Youth complexion for a few moments. I babbled aimlessly to myself and then managed to pull together and beat it to the lake with as much speed as my farmer friend had shown in his retreat. I made the boat and the hotel in double quick time.

I felt no misgivings now as to the promise of a sensation that night, and that sustaining thought was all that propped my flagging spirits throughout the day, but I resolved to keep my little party at safe distance from the house.

"Say we keep our nocturnal noctambulation under our hats," proposed Rob.

When this proposition was translated to Silvia, she entirely approved, so, committing Diogenes to the Polydores' Providence, we left the hotel at half past eleven for a row on the lake by moonlight.

When we descended the slope leading to the House of Mystery, I cautioned silence and a "safety-first" distance.

"Ghosts are easily vanished," I informed them. "They don't seek limelight, and I want you to be sure to see this one."

As we came to the untrodden undergrowth we heard a weird, wailing sound that would have curdled my blood had I not glanced in the window that afternoon and so, in a measure, been prepared for this—or anything.

"Look!" whispered Beth. "The arm!"

Silvia looked at the roof window and with a stifled shriek of terror turned and fled up the hill, Rob chivalrously pursuing her.

Beth was pale, but game.

"What can it be, Lucien?" she whispered. "Do we dare go in to see?"

"I wouldn't, Beth," I vetoed quickly. "Maybe some lunatic or half-witted person has taken up abode here."

"Lucien!" called Rob peremptorily.

I turned quickly. He was at the top of the hill, half supporting Silvia. I ran toward them, followed by Beth.

"It isn't a ghost, of course, Silvia," I said soothingly, and then repeated my supposition about the lunatic.

"Of course I don't believe in ghosts," said Silvia shudderingly, "but it's an awful place and those sounds are like those I have heard in nightmares."

"We'll hurry back to the hotel and forget all about it," I urged.

I rowed the boat and Silvia sat opposite me. Beth and Rob were in the stern and I had to listen to their conversation.

"Of course I felt a little creepy," she admitted, "but then I like to feel that way, and I wasn't afraid."

"No, of course, you wouldn't be," he replied somewhat ironically. "You're the new woman type."

"No, I am not," she denied. "I wish I were. Silvia's really the strong-minded type."

"She didn't act the part when she saw the ghost," he retorted.

"It's very unusual for her nerves to give way. Silvia's quite a surprise to me this summer, but I think those funny Polydores have upset her more than Lucien realizes."

I wondered if she were right, and once again murderous wishes toward the Polydores entered my brain, and I made renewed vows about disposing of them on our return home.

One thing, however, had been accomplished by our expedition. Silvia was more lenient in her judgment on my indulgences of the preceding night.

By the time we pulled in at the landing, Silvia had recovered her equilibrium.

"Lucien, what the devil do you suppose was in that house?" asked Rob, when we were putting up the boat.

"Loons and things," I allowed.

"But what was that white arm?"

"Some fake thing the village wag has put up to scare the natives."

Next morning's stage brought some new arrivals, and among them were two college students who at once were claimed by Beth. She played tennis with one and later went rowing with the other. Rob smoked and sulked, apart.

My farmer friend had been garrulous and rumors of the ghost and the haunted house had come to the ears of the hotel inmates, thereby causing a pleasurable stir of excitement. A number of them announced their intention of visiting the place. They asked me to be their guide, but I refused.

"It was interesting," I said, "but I think it would be a bore to see the same ghost twice."

"I am sure I don't care to go again," was Silvia's emphatic reply when asked to be one of the party.

"Ghosts are scientifically admitted and explained," growled Rob, "so I don't see anything to be excited about."

Beth accepted the offer of escort of one of the students, so Silvia, Rob, and I remained at home. The night was quite cool, and we played cards in our room. When the party returned, Beth joined us. She looked rather out of sorts.

"Oh, yes," she replied in answer to Silvia's eager inquiry. "We saw the ghost. I don't know whether it was the same little old last night's ghost or a new one. He showed more of himself this time though. He had two arms and a veiled head out of the window. As soon as our crowd glimpsed it, they all fled quicker than we did last night. Those two students fell all over each other and left me in the lurch."

"What could you expect," asked Rob, "from such ladylike things? They ought to be kept in the confines of the croquet ground. If they are a fair specimen of the kind you have met, no wonder you—"

He stopped abruptly.

"No wonder what?" she asked quickly.

"Nothing," he replied glumly.

When I came down to breakfast the next morning, the landlady in tears waylaid me.

"Oh, Mr. Wade," she began in trouble-telling tone, "this affair about the ghost is going to hurt my business. Some of those folks say they are going home, and they will tell others and—"

"I'll fix the ghost story. Just leave it to me!" I assured her optimistically, as we went into the dining-room.

There were only enough guests to fill one long table, and every one was excitedly dissecting the ghost.

I took my seat and also the floor.

"I hate to dispel your illusions," I said cheerfully, "but the fact is, I made a daylight investigation of the haunted house. First I looked in the window and I saw—"

"Oh, what did you see?" chorused a dozen or more expectant voices.

"A lot of—mice."

"Oh!" came in disappointed and skeptical tones.

"But, the ghost, Mr. Wade?"

"Yes! The arms and the head?"

"A fake figure put up by some practical joker for the purpose of frightening timid people and encouraging the credulous. I didn't want to spoil your little picnic, so I kept still."

"Those sounds, Lucien!" reminded Silvia.

"Were from a cat chorus. They were prowling about the house."

"You're sure some lawyer, Mr. Wade," doubtfully complimented my grateful landlady, as we went out of the room after breakfast.

"Lucien," asked Rob *sotto voce*, joining me on the veranda, "why don't the cats you speak of catch that lot of mice?"

Fortunately Beth came up to us, and I didn't have to explain.

"Oh!" she said with a shudder. "I'll never go near that awful place! I'd rather see a perfectly good ghost, or a loon, or a lunatic any day than a mouse."

"You're surely not afraid of a mouse!" exclaimed Rob.

"Why not?" she asked coolly as she walked on.

"I told you she was feminine," I reminded him.

He shook his head.

"I can't understand," he remarked, "why a girl who is afraid of mice should be—"

"You don't understand anything about women," I interrupted.

"You're right, Lucien. I don't, but your sister is surely the greatest enigma of them all."

I rented the stone fence farmer's "autoo" and took Silvia and Diogenes to a neighboring town that afternoon. We didn't get back to the hotel until dinner time.

"What have you been up to all day, Rob?" I asked.

"Numerous things. For one, I strolled down to the haunted house."

"What did you see?" cried the women.

"I saw four—"

"Ghosts?" asked Beth.

I shot him a warning glance.

"Young tomcats playing tag with the mice."

I corralled Rob outside after dinner.

"For Heaven's sake!" I implored. "Don't disturb Silvia's peace of mind. Did you go inside?"

"No; I was sorely tempted to, but refrained out of deference to the evident wishes of my host, but really, Lucien, we should—"

"I have only ten more days off, Rob. Don't make any unpleasant suggestions."

"I won't," he said promptly.

# X

## In Which We Make Some Discoveries

Diogenes, who, for a Polydore, had been quite placid since Ptolemy's departure, caused a commotion by disappearing the next morning. As he was possessed of a deep desire to go in the lake and get a little snake, he had been, when not under strict surveillance, tied to a tree with enough leeway in the length of rope to allow him to play comfortably.

By some means he had managed to work himself loose from the rope and had evidently followed Ptolemy's example. I suggested calling up Huldah and asking if he had arrived yet, but I met with such chilling glances from Silvia and Beth that I got busy and organized searching parties, who reluctantly and lukewarmly engaged in the pursuit. Rob and I took the shore. After we had walked some little distance, we met a woman and stopped for inquiry. She said she had seen a child of about two years, clad in a blue and white striped dress and a big hat, going over the hill in company with a boy of about eight.

"Are you going on to the hotel?" I asked.

On her replying that she was, I told her to inform them that she had met me and that the lost child was located.

Rob and I then kept on over the hill, and when we neared the haunted house, we heard hair-raising sounds.

"If I hadn't been here before," remarked Rob, "I should think that Sitting Bull had been reincarnated and was reviving the warrior war whoops."

We paused on the threshold. A human windmill of whirling legs and arms—Polydore legs and arms—flashed before our eyes.

"Stop!" I thundered.

The flying wheel of arms and legs slacked, ran a few times, then slowly stopped, and the Polydore quintette assumed normal positions.

"Halloa, stepdaddy!"

A landslide composed of Emerald, Pythagoras, and Demetrius started toward me. I side-stepped and let Rob receive the charge.

"Line them up now, for attention," I directed Ptolemy. "I have something to say to you all."

Ptolemy knocked the three terrors up against the wall, and I picked up Diogenes, who had a bump as big as an egg on his head.

"I told you," said Ptolemy to Pythagoras, "that if you brought Di down here they'd get on our trail. He wanted to see Di," he explained, "so he sneaked over there and got him."

"We were wise before today," I informed him. "I saw you all day before yesterday."

"And I discovered you yesterday," added Rob.

Ptolemy looked rather crestfallen, and then, seeming to consider that my discovery had been succeeded by inaction, which must mean non-interference, he heartened up.

"Now," I demanded, "I want you to begin at the time you left the hotel and tell me everything and why you did it."

"I wasn't having any fun after you two went off camping," he began lugubriously. "I couldn't hang around women folks all the time. I wanted boys to play with."

I saw a gleam of sympathy and understanding come into Rob's eyes.

"A harem of hens," he muttered.

"I knew we could all have a grand time here and not be a bother to mudder, or Huldah or anyone, and it seemed too bad for this nice house to be empty, and no one anywhere else wanting us."

I felt my first gleam of pity for a Polydore and wiped Diogenes' dirty, moist face carefully with my handkerchief.

"So I went home and told Huldah I had come after the boys to take them back with me."

"And told her we had sent for them?" I asked sharply.

He flushed slightly at my tone.

"No; I didn't tell her so. She got that idea herself, and I didn't tell her different."

"When did you come?"

"I came the same night that you telephoned, and took the train you and mudder came on. We got to Windy Creek in the morning. We fetched all our stuff here from home. I bought it."

"Right here," I said, "tell me where you got the money to buy your stuff and to pay your fare here."

"I cashed father's check."

"I didn't know he left you one."

"He didn't, except the one he gave me to give you for our board. You told mudder you wouldn't touch it, and it seemed a pity not to have it working."

Visions of a future Polydore doing the chain and ball step flashed before my vision.

"And they cashed it for you at the bank?"

"Sure. Father always has me cash his checks for him."

"What amount did you fill in?" I asked enviously.

"One hundred dollars. There's a lot more in the bank, too."

"How did you get your truck here from Windy Creek?" asked Rob.

"We divided it up and each took a bunch and started on foot, and some people in an automobile, going to the town past here, took us in and brought us as far as the lane. We've been having a fine time."

"What doing?" asked Rob interestedly.

"Fishing, sailing on a raft, playing in the woods all day and—"

"Playing ghost at night," said Pythagoras with a grin.

"Who made that ghost in the window?" I demanded.

"I did. I rigged up an arm and put it out the window the afternoon I left, hoping Beth would come down and see it, but we've got a jim dandy one now."

"That was quite a shapely arm," said Rob. "Where did you learn sculpturing?"

"Oh, I rigged it up," he said casually.

"What did you bring in the way of supplies?"

"Bacon, crackers, beans, candy, popcorn, gum, peanuts, pickles, candles, matches, and butter," was the glib inventory.

"You may stay here," I said, "until we go home, but you are not to stir away from the woods about here and not on any account to come near the hotel, or let it be known that you are here. And you are to end this ghost business right off. Now, Di, we'll go home to mudder."

"No!" bawled Di. "Stay with boys. Mudder come here."

At least this was Ptolemy's interpretation of his protest.

I threatened, Rob coaxed, and Ptolemy cuffed, but every time I started to leave and jerk him after me, he uttered such demoniac yells I was forced to stop.

"Wish it was night," said Emerald regretfully. "Wouldn't he scare folks though! How does he get his voice up so high?"

"Poor little Di!" said a voice commiseratingly from the doorway. "Was Ocean plaguing him?"

Beth gathered the child in her arms, and his howls changed to sobs. Rob stood petrified with amazement at her appearance.

"Don't want to go," said Diogenes between gulps.

"Needn't go!" promised Beth. "Stay here with me, and we'll have dinner with the boys and then we'll go home and get some ice cream."

"All yite," agreed the appeased Polydore.

"May Lucien and I stay to dinner, too?" asked Rob humbly.

"No," she replied icily.

"But, Beth," I remonstrated. "Silvia will be worrying about Di. How can we explain?"

"Silvia has gone to Windy Creek for the day. You see, I met that woman you sent to the hotel, and she told me she saw Di going over the hill with a boy, and I suddenly seemed to smell one of your mice, so I sent the woman on her way, and told Silvia you and Rob had found Diogenes. Just then some people she knew came along in a car and asked her to go to Windy Creek. I made her go and told her I'd look after Di."

"You're a brick, Beth!" applauded Ptolemy.

"If you boys will be very careful and not let anyone besides us know you are here, so mudder will not hear of it, for though she'd like to see you"—this without a flicker or flinch—"we want her to have a nice rest. I'll come over every day except tomorrow and bring things from the hotel store, and bake up cookies and cake for you."

A yell of approval went up.

"Why can't you come tomorrow?" asked the greedy Demetrius.

"Because I've promised to go to the other end of the lake on a picnic. All the people at the hotel are going."

"I'll come tomorrow and spend the whole day with you," promised Rob. "We'll have a ride in the sailboat and do all sorts of things."

"Why, aren't you going on that infernal picnic?" I asked.

"No; I'll have all the picnic I want over here. Like Ptolemy I feel that I want to play with some of my own kind."

Beth looked at him approvingly; then she said a little sarcastically:

"Maybe you'll change your mind—about going on the picnic, I mean—when you see the new girl who just came to the hotel on the morning stage. She's a blonde, and not peroxided, either."

"That would certainly drive him down here, or anywhere," I laughed.

"Oh, don't you like blondes?" she asked innocently.

"He doesn't like—" I began, but Ptolemy rudely interrupted with an elaborate description of a new kind of fishing tackle he had bought.

Then Beth bade Pythagoras build a fire in the cookstove while she set the room to rights.

"We'll eat out of doors," she said, "I think it would be more appetizing."

"How did you get here?" Rob asked her as we were leaving.

"I rowed over."

"May I come over and row you back?" he asked pleadingly.

She hesitated, and then, realizing that she could scarcely manage a boat and Diogenes at the same time, assented, bidding him not come, however, until five o'clock.

"She'll have enough of the Polydores by that time," I said to Rob on our way home.

"Do you know," he said reflectively, "I like Ptolemy. There's the making of a man in him, if he has only half a chance. I didn't suppose your sister understood children so well or was so fond of them. She looked quite the little housewife, too."

"You'd discover a lot of things you don't know, if you'd cultivate the society of women," I informed him.

# XI

## A Bad Means to a Good End

When we were setting out on the proposed picnic the next day, Rob made himself extremely unpopular by announcing his intention to spend the day otherwise. The new blonde girl gave him fetching glances of entreaty which he never even saw. He made another sensation by proposing to keep Diogenes with him. To Silvia's surprise, Diogenes voiced his delight and chattered away, I suppose, about playing with the boys, but fortunately no one understood him.

"Won't you change your mind and come, too?" he asked Beth.

She seemed on the point of accepting and then firmly declined.

When we returned at six o'clock, Rob and Diogenes were awaiting us. There was something in Rob's eyes I had not seen there before. He had the look of one in love with life.

"Did you have a nice time playing solitaire?" asked Silvia.

"I had a very nice time," he replied with a subtle smile, "but I didn't play solitaire. You know I had Diogenes."

"Diogenes apparently had a good time, too," said Silvia, looking at the child, who was certainly a wreck in the way of garments. "What did you do all day, Rob?"

"We went out on the water, played games, and had a picnic dinner outdoors."

"You had huckleberry pie for one thing," she observed, with a glance at Diogenes' dress, "and jelly for another, and—"

"Chicken, baked potatoes, milk, cake, and ice cream," he finished.

"Where did you get ice cream?" she asked.

"I went down to a dairy farm and got a gallon."

"A gallon!" she exclaimed. "For you and Diogenes?"

"We didn't eat it all," he said guardedly. "I gave what we didn't eat to some stray boys."

"I hope Di won't be ill."

"He won't," asserted Rob. "I am sure he is made of cast iron."

Throughout dinner Rob remained in high spirits. He kept eyeing Beth in a way that disconcerted her, and then suddenly he would smile with the expression of one who knows something funny, but intends to keep it a secret.

Presently Silvia left us and went upstairs to give Diogenes a bath before she put him to bed.

"You've had two days' freedom from the last of the Polydores," I called after her. "Doesn't it seem delightful?"

"Lucien," she answered slowly, "I've really missed the care of him. I was lonesome for him all day."

"He isn't such a bad little kid when he is out from Polydore environment," I admitted, regretting that he had been restored to it.

"Now tell us all about your day with the boys," Beth asked Rob, when we were left alone. "It really does seem too bad to keep a secret from Silvia, and yet it is a case of where ignorance is bliss—"

"It would be folly to be otherwise," finished Rob. "Well, Diogenes and I left here with a boat load of supplies in the way of provender and things for the boys. I had to tie Diogenes in the boat, of course, so he would not try some aquatic feat. He objected and yelled like a fiend all the way. I was glad there was no one at the hotel to come out and arrest me for cruelty to children. Of course before we landed, his cries were heard by his brothers and they were all at the water's edge. They made mulepacks of themselves and transferred the commissary supplies. The ice cream and bats and balls which I found at the store made quite a hit.

"We played baseball, fished, and had a spread on the shore. Then Ptolemy and I rowed out to where the sailboat was. I explained the mysteries of the jib and he caught on instantly. We took in the other Polydores and sailed for a couple of hours. Then we all went in swimming."

"Not Diogenes!"

"Certainly. I tucked him under my arm and he seemed perfectly at home, although greatly disappointed because we didn't succeed in catching a snake.

"I finally landed them all safely under the roof of the Haunted House, and Ptolemy assured me it was the best day of his young life. In appreciation of the diversions I had afforded him, he made a confession which proved such good news to me that I was a lenient listener and exacted no penalty."

"What was it?" I asked.

"He told me that on the day of Miss Wade's and my arrival at your house, he had made a misstatement to each of us and had not repeated to us accurately what he had overheard you telling Silvia when he was on the porch roof. Miss Wade, what did he tell you about me?"

"He said that Lucien said that your only failing was that you were daffy over women and made love to every one you saw."

"Oh, Beth!" I cried, light bursting in, "and you believed that little wretch?"

"I did."

"Then that is why you have been so—"

"Yes—so—," repeated Rob grimly.

"Well, I never did have any use for a man-flirt, and I was awfully disappointed, for I had thought from what Rob said that you were a man's man."

"And then, of course, when for the first time in my life I began being interested in a woman—in you—I played right into that little scamp's hands."

"He is a man's man, Beth," I said warmly. "What Ptolemy heard me say was that Rob was a woman-hater."

"I am not!" declared Rob indignantly—"just a woman-shyer, but I haven't finished with Ptolemy's confession. I wonder, now, if either of you can guess what he told me was Miss Wade's characteristic."

"I don't dare guess," laughed Beth.

"What I did say about Beth was that she was a born flirt."

"I am not!" protested my sister, in resentment.

"I should prefer that appellation to the one he gave you. He said you were strong-minded and a man-hater."

Even Beth saw the irony of this.

"I asked him," continued Rob, "what his motive was, and he said 'Stepdaddy didn't want Beth to know about the man-hater business,' so he took that means of throwing you off the track.

"I took the occasion to talk to him like a Dutch uncle, though I don't know exactly what that is. I think it was the first time anything but brute force had been tried on him. I must have touched some little flicker of the right thing in him, for he was really contrite and seemed to sense a different angle of vision when I explained to him what havoc could be worked by the misinformation of meddlers. He promised me he'd try to overcome his tendency to start things going wrong."

I made no comment, but it occurred to me that Ptolemy was a shrewd little fellow, and that there had been wisdom back of his strategic speeches to Beth and Rob, for he had taken the one sure course to make them both "take notice."

"So, Beth," said Rob, and her name seemed to come quite handily to him, "can't we cut out the past ten days and begin our acquaintance right?"

"I think we can," she answered.

"I had better go upstairs," I suggested, "and tell Silvia that Diogenes doesn't need a bath, seeing he has been in swimming."

Neither of them urged me to remain, so I went up to our room and found Silvia tucking Diogenes under cover.

"What did you come up for?" she asked. "I was just coming down to join you."

"Beth is treating Rob so—differently, that I thought it well to retreat."

"I am so glad! Whatever came over the spirit of her dreams?"

"They've just discovered in the course of conversation that Ptolemy as usual crossed the wires and told Beth Rob was a flirt, and then informed Rob that Beth was strong-minded and a man-hater."

"Oh, the little imp!" she exclaimed indignantly.

"I don't know. It worked, anyway, so Ptolemy was the bad means to a good end."

"How did they ever happen to discover what he had done?"

"They caught on from something Rob said," I told her, feeling again guilty at keeping my first secret from her.

"It will be a fine match for Beth," said Silvia. "Rob is such a splendid man, and then he has plenty of money. He can give her anything she wants."

I winced. I think Silvia must have been conscious of it, even though the room was dark, for she came to me quickly.

"I wish I could give you—everything—anything—you want, Silvia."

"You have, Lucien. The things that no money could buy—love and protection."

Well, maybe I had. I had surely given her protection from the Polydores, though she didn't know to what extent.

"I am going to give you more material things, though, Silvia. When we go home, I shall start to work in earnest and see if I can't get enough ahead to make a good investment I know of."

"I'd rather do without the necessities even, Lucien, than to have you work any harder than you have been doing. We must let well enough alone."

# XII

# "Too Much Polydores"

The next morning at breakfast, Beth announced that she and Rob were going to spend the day camping in the woods.

Silvia and I tried not to look significantly at each other, but Beth was very keen.

"We will take Diogenes with us," she instantly added.

"Oh, no!" protested Silvia. "He'll be such a bother. And then he can't walk very far, you know."

"He'll be no bother," persisted Beth. "And we'll borrow the little cart to draw him in."

"Yes," acquiesced Rob. "We sure want Diogenes with us."

"I'll have them put up a lunch for you," proposed Silvia.

"No," Rob objected. "We are going to forage and cook over a fire in the woods."

"Then," I proposed to Silvia with alacrity, "we'll have our first day alone together—the first we have had since the Polydores came into our lives. I'll rent the 'autoo' again, and we will go through the country and dine at some little wayside inn."

"Get the 'autoo,' now, Lucien," advised Beth privately, "and make an early start, so Rob and I can take supplies from the store without arousing Silvia's suspicions."

"I don't believe," said Silvia disappointedly, when we were "autooing" on our way, "that they are in love after all, or that he has proposed, or that he is going to."

"Where did you draw all those pessimistic inferences from?" I asked.

"From their both being so keen to take Diogenes with them."

"Diogenes would be no barrier to their love-making," I told her. "He couldn't repeat what they said; at least, not so anyone could understand him."

Many miles away we came upon a picturesque little old-time tavern where we had an appetizing dinner, and then continued on our aimless way. It was nearly ten o'clock when we returned to the hotel, where the owner of the "autoo" was waiting.

Rob came down the roadway.

"Where's Beth?" asked Silvia.

"She has gone to bed. The day in the open made her sleepy."

When Silvia had left us, the old farmer said with a chuckle: "I can't offer you another swig of stone fence."

"It's probably just as well you can't," I replied.

"I'd like to be introduced to one," said Rob, who appeared to be somewhat downcast. "I sure need a bracer."

"What's the matter, Rob?" I asked when we were lighting our pipes. "A strenuous day? Two in rapid 'concussion' with the Polydores must be nerve-racking."

"Yes; I admit there seemed to be 'too much Polydores.' We all had a happy reunion, and I devoted the forenoon to the entertainment of the famous family so I could be entitled to the afternoon off to spend with Beth. At noon we built a fire and cooked a sumptuous dinner. Beth baked up some things to keep them supplied a couple of days longer. After dinner I asked her to go for a row. She insisted on taking Diogenes along, and the others all followed us on a raft. So I decided to cut the water sports short, and Beth and I started for a walk in the woods. Three or more were constantly right on our trail. I begged and bribed, but to no avail. They were sticktights all right, and," he added morosely, "she seemed covertly to aid and abet them. When we started for home, I found that the young fiends had broken the cart, so I had to carry Diogenes most of the way, and of course he bellowed as usual at being parted from the whelps."

"They aren't such 'fine little chaps' after all," I couldn't resist commenting. "Familiarity breeds contempt, you see. I am sorry Diogenes had so much of their society. He'll be unendurable tomorrow. Well, you had some day!"

"So did the Polydores. Demetrius and Diogenes fell in the fire twice. Emerald threw a finger out of joint, but Ptolemy quickly jerked it into place. Pythagoras was kicked off the raft twice, following a mutiny. Demetrius threw a lighted match into the vines and set fire to the house. They said it was a 'beaut of a day,' though, and urged us to come tomorrow and repeat the program. By the way, they went across the lake on their raft yesterday and bought a tent of some campers. They have pitched it in the woods beyond the house."

When I went upstairs Silvia met me disconsolately.

"He didn't propose," she said disappointedly. "She wouldn't let him."

"Did you wake her up to find out?" I asked.

"She hadn't gone to bed and she wasn't sleepy. She was trimming a hat."

"Why wouldn't she let him propose, if she cares for him?" I asked perplexedly.

"Well, you see," explained Silvia, "that when a girl—a coquette girl like Beth—is as sure of a man as she is of Rob, she gets a touch of contrariness or offishness or something. She said it would have been too prosaic and cut and dried if they had gone away for a day in the woods and come back engaged. She wants the unexpected."

"Do you think she loves him?" I asked interestedly.

"She doesn't say so. You can't tell from what she says anyway. Still, I think she is hovering around the danger point."

"She'd better watch out. Rob isn't the kind of a man who will stand for too much thwarting," I replied.

"If he'd only play up a little bit to some one else, it would bring things to a climax," said my wife sagely.

"There's no one else to play up to. The blonde left today because it was so slow here."

"Maybe some new girl will come tomorrow," said Silvia, "or there's that trim little waitress who is waiting her way through college. He gave her a good big tip yesterday. I think I will give him a hint."

"It wouldn't help any. He wouldn't know how to play such a game if you could persuade him to try. He'd probably tell the girl his motive in being attentive to her and then she'd back out. Maybe, after all, Beth doesn't love him."

"I think she does," replied my wife, "because she is getting absent-minded. She let Diogenes go too near the fire. His shoes are burned, his hair singed, and his dress scorched. He woke up when I came in and he was so cross. He acted just the way he does when he is with his brothers."

# XIII

## Rob's Friend the Reporter

Silvia's vague prophecy was fulfilled. When the event of the day, the arrival of the stage, occurred, a solitary passenger alighted, a slim, alert, city-cut young woman.

She looked us all over—not boldly, but with a business-like directness as if she were taking inventory of stock, or acting as judge at a competition. When her blue eyes lighted on Rob, they darkened with pleasure.

"Oh, Mr. Rossiter!" she exclaimed, "this is better than I hoped for."

They shook hands with the air of being old acquaintances, and he introduced her to us as "Miss Frayne, from my home town."

She went into the office, registered, and sent her bag to her room. Then she asked Rob if she might have a talk with him.

They walked away together down to the shore and she was talking to him quite excitedly. Rob suddenly stopped, threw back his head and laughed in the way that it is good to hear a man laugh.

"Miss Frayne must be a wit," observed Beth dryly.

I looked at her keenly. Something in her eyes as she gazed after the retreating couple told me that Silvia's surmise was right, and that Miss Frayne might be just the little punch needed to send Beth over the danger point.

"I rather incline to the belief that Ptolemy told the truth in the first place," she continued, and then looked disappointed because I did not contradict her.

I decided not to reveal, for the present anyway, what I knew of Miss Frayne, of whom I had often heard Rob speak.

"She can't be going to stay long," said Silvia hopefully. "She didn't bring a trunk."

"She doesn't need one," replied Beth. "She is probably one of those mannish girls who believe in a skirt and a few waists for a wardrobe."

When Rob and the newcomer returned, he seemed to be monopolizing the conversation in a very emphatic and earnest manner. As they came up the steps to the veranda, we heard her say:

"Very well, Mr. Rossiter, I will do just as you say. I have perfect confidence in your judgment."

They passed on into the hotel and Beth jumped up and went down toward the lake.

"Did you ever hear Rob speak of this Miss Frayne?" asked Silvia.

"Often. She is engaged to his cousin, and is a reporter on a big newspaper."

"Why didn't you say so? Oh, Lucien," she continued before I could speak, "were you really shrewd enough to see which way the wind was blowing?"

"Sure. After you set my sails for me last night."

Just then Rob came out of the hotel.

"Say, Lucien, I want to see you a minute. Come on down the road."

"We've got some work ahead," he said when we were out of Silvia's hearing.

"What's up?" I asked.

"Miss Frayne is up—and doing. What do you suppose her paper sent her here for?"

"For a rest, or to write up the mosquitoes of H. H."

"H. H. is all right, only it happens they stand for Haunted House."

"Not really?"

"Yes, really. The rumors of the house and the ghost, greatly elaborated, of course, reached the Sunday editor of the paper Miss Frayne is on, and he sent her up here to revive the story of the murder, translate the ghost, and get snapshots of the house. She was quite keen to have me take her there at once, so she could commence her article, but I headed her off, so she wouldn't discover the summer boarders at the hotel annex. I assured her that daytime was not the time to gather material and the only way she could get a proper focus on the ghost and acquire the thrills necessary for an inspiration was to see the place first by night."

"If she would view Fair Melrose aright," I quoted, "she must visit it in the pale moonlight, but you were very clever to delay her visit long enough for us to get over there and warn the enemy. If she had gone down there and caught the Polydores unawares, she would have come back here and revealed our secret, and there would be the end of Silvia's vacation."

"To tell the truth, Lucien, I wasn't thinking so much of that as I was of Miss Frayne's interests. You see she has come a long ways for a story and if it collapsed from her ghostly expectations to a showdown of four healthy boys, the blow might mean a good deal to her in a business way. I think we had better let Ptolemy plant a ghost just once more for her. You know you made him take a reef in the flapping of ghostly garments. Can't we resurrect the specter and restore the wails just for tonight, and bring her over here at the witching hour?"

"Sure we will," I agreed heartily. "She shall have her ghost and all the trappings. It will give the Polydores the time of their lives."

"Let's go over there now and put Ptolemy next so he can get busy on his spirits." We went down to the shore and pulled off. Midway across the lake, Rob suddenly rested on his oars and asked:

"Where did Beth go?"

"Back to first principles," I replied. "She thinks, judging from your excited, earnest manner in addressing Miss Frayne and your rushing frantically away for a walk with her before she had removed the travel dust, that

Ptolemy was quite correct, after all, in declaring you to be a 'ladies' man.'"

"Didn't you explain to her who Miss Frayne was?" he asked.

"No," I replied. "I am on my vacation and I am not doing any explaining, professionally or otherwise."

He swung the boat around.

"Starboard!" I cried. "Don't you know a trump card when you see it?"

Again he rested on his oars and stared at me.

"What do you mean, Lucien? If you have a grain of hope for me, please let me in."

I repeated Silvia's theories.

"I am not going to win her that way," he said slowly, "not by playing a part."

"Well," I declared, "if you go back to the hotel now, you can't explain Miss Frayne to Beth, because she went for a walk with old Professor Treadtop."

He turned the boat again.

"Silvia won't come to the Haunted House, will she?" he asked.

"No, indeed. Nothing would induce her to."

"Then you bring Miss Frayne here tonight and I'll bring Beth. And I'll be sure that there are no double boats lying around loose. I'll have two at the dock, see?"

"I see your system," I replied, "but I am not sure how I can explain Miss Frayne to Silvia. Silvia is not in the least narrow-minded, but still to leave the hotel at midnight with a perfectly strange young woman—"

"You can tell her I want a clear field for Beth. She will see it is in a good cause."

The Polydores greeted us rapturously and roughly. When I had restored order, and they were once more right side up, I addressed the chief of the bandits.

"Ptolemy," I began, "a young lady, who is a reporter for a big newspaper, has come from many miles away to write up the haunted house and the ghost, and they will be pictured out in the Sunday edition."

Ptolemy's eyes glistened, and "Them Three" were instantly "at attention."

"Oh, say, stepdaddy," begged the young chief, "let me play ghost right for her, just once, will you?"

"You may for tonight," I said, "but you will have to be very careful and not overdo the matter, for she isn't the kind that is easily fooled. She's had to keep her eyes and wits sharpened, else she wouldn't be on a newspaper, so I want you to be very careful and not bungle. Make a neat job of it."

"I'll do it up brown, you bet!" he cried gleefully.

"Naw, do it up white," drawled Pythagoras.

"Show me your ghost stuff by daylight," I demanded, "and let me see how you are going to rig him up."

He brought forth a head and shoulders and arms that were ghastly even in sunlight, and proceeded to explain them.

"I got this skull out of father's study, and the arms came off a skeleton mother had in her antiquities. I dressed them up in a pillow case and the white cotton gloves are Huldah's. I can get some phosphorus in the woods and put it in the eyes. And Demetrius bought two electric flashlights yesterday, and Pythagoras can snap them once in a while from the lower windows."

"You are some little property man," said Rob in admiration. "But tell me who produces those heart-rending shrieks?"

"That was Pythagoras who did the high ones. And Em came in with low groans. Show 'em, boys."

Pythagoras uttered high-trebled, thin-toned whines and ever and anon Emerald added a *basso profundo* accompaniment, making a combination that was most trying to the ears at close range.

"I don't know," said Rob, "as I want Beth subjected to such a realistic performance. We will loiter in the distance."

"Your rehearsal," I assured Ptolemy, "is very good, but you must remember that Miss Frayne is used to encountering things far more terrible than ghosts. She may insist on coming right in here to investigate. Of course, if she does, I can't refuse or she'll think I am afraid, or else that I put up a fake ghost here, myself."

"We'll lock the door with a chair," suggested Emerald.

"She'll be quite capable of breaking into a little house like this, but I'll keep her back until you have time to haul in your ghost and make a quick and quiet getaway by a back window. Then another thing, she'll be over here tomorrow morning to take some pictures of the house, so by sunrise I want you all to take up your abode in the tent you have in the woods and stay there until I come and tell you the coast is clear."

"We're dead on," assured Ptolemy. "I'm glad there's going to be something doing. We're getting tired of being here alone. I had to tie Demetrius up this morning. He was bound to go over to the hotel and see mudder."

"Don't one of you dare to make such an attempt," I said peremptorily. "You keep right on here for a few days. Some of us, either Rob, or Beth and I will drop over every day. If you play your ghost just as I tell you and keep out of sight, I'll bring you over some ice cream tomorrow."

"Bring me a bigger bat."

"Bring me a mitt."

"Bring me a boat," came in chorus from Ptolemy, Emerald, and Demetrius.

"What'll you give me to stay here?" asked Pythagoras, who was a born bargain-driver.

"I'll give you a licking if you don't stay," was the only offer he gleaned from me.

"Be good boys," adjured the softhearted Rob, "and I'll bring you everything I can find at the hotel."

It was long past the luncheon hour when we returned. We found Miss Frayne wondering at Rob's sudden disappearance and Beth was accordingly mystified.

I planted myself directly in front of Miss Frayne.

"May I take you to the haunted house tonight at the yawning churchyard hour?" I asked. "I am most eminently fitted to be your guide, for I was the first one of this assembly to see the ghost *in toto*."

"He saw it over a stone fence," remarked Rob.

"Indeed you may, thank you very much," she said enthusiastically.

Silvia's face was a study.

"And will you come with me, Beth?" asked Rob. "Of course, the ghost is an old story to us, but we really should hover in Lucien's wake out of regard to the conventions."

"Is Miss Frayne interested in ghosts?" asked Beth.

Miss Frayne turned and answered the question.

"Not personally," she admitted frankly, "but the newspaper I am on is, and they sent me up here to get a story."

"Oh, you are a reporter?"

"Yes; on the *Times*."

"She won't be one long, though," asserted Rob cheerfully, "because she is going to marry my cousin in the fall."

Beth's expression remained neutral at the announcement, but I noticed throughout the afternoon that she was extremely affable toward Miss Frayne, and that she had the whiphand again with Rob, and meanwhile he seemed to be gathering a grim determination to do or die.

"Lucien, how did you come to ask Miss Frayne to go to that awful place tonight?" asked Silvia when we had gone to our room for a siesta, which seemed impossible by reason of the bellowing of Diogenes, who balked at being required to lie down.

"Rob asked me to," I informed her, when I had cowed Diogenes, "so he could have a free field for Beth. I believe he planned this expedition so he could storm the citadel."

She reflected.

"Well, maybe he is wise. Girls like Beth have to be taken by storm sometimes. I shouldn't wonder if Rob could be a bit of a bully, too, but—"

She ended her speculations in a shriek.

"Oh, Lucien! Diogenes has jumped out the window."

We rushed down stairs, Silvia informing the guests in transit of the awful catastrophe.

Silvia paused at the door opening on to the veranda.

"I can't see him," she said faintly, closing her eyes. "You'll have to tend to it alone, Lucien."

Beth was already at the telephone, which connected with the country doctor's. Rob joined me. We located our window, and began hunting underneath for the pieces.

"Where in the world do you suppose he landed?" asked Rob.

Just then the missing one came around the house clasping a bologna sausage in his fist.

"Ye Gods and little Polydores!" exclaimed Rob.

I caught Diogenes by the arm and rushed him in to Silvia.

I found her in company with an old colored mammy, who was laundress for the hotel.

"Sho'," she was saying, "I done gwine by de windah with ma baby cab full o' cloes, an' dis yer white chile done come tumblin' down an' fall right in ma cab. Now, what do you think o' dat? I reckon I was nevah so done clean skeert afoah in ma life. An' ef de chile didn't grab one of ma bolognas and done git out de cab an' run around de house."

"Oh," cried Silvia, "poor little baby! Come to mudder. Lucien, where are you going with him?"

I had picked up the acrobatic Polydore and was going up the stairs two at a time. I gained our room, locked the door and proceeded to give the "poor little baby" all that was coming to him. Now and then above his howls, I heard Silvia's plaintive protests outside the door, but I finished my job completely and satisfactorily, and laid the penitent Polydore in his little bed. Then I went out into the hall, feeling better than I had in months.

Silvia essayed to pass me, but I took her arm and led her to a recess in the hall.

"I am convinced," I told her, "that we have Diogenes as a permanent pensioner on our hands, so it was up to me to show him where to get off. You can't go to him for a quarter of an hour."

We went down stairs and I was sure I read suppressed regret in the faces of most of the guests at learning of the soft place in which Diogenes' lot had been cast. Silvia tearfully told Rob and Beth of my cruelty.

"Do him good!" approved Rob heartily.

"How mean men are!" declared Beth indignantly. "I am going up and comfort the poor little thing."

I held up the key to the room with a grin, and she had to content herself by making unkind remarks about me.

At the expiration of the allotted time, I handed Silvia the key. She took it from me without a word or a look. It was quite evident I was in wrong.

In half an hour my wife came down, carrying Diogenes, who, dressed in fresh white clothes, was a good picture of an angel child. She passed me and went to a remote corner of the veranda and sat down. When he spied me, he leaped from her arms and ran to me.

"Ocean," he said propitiatingly, "me love oo."

I took him up. His arms clasped about my neck, and over his curly head, I winked at Silvia and Beth.

Rob roared.

# XIV

## A Midnight Excursion

The night was Satan's own: dark, wind-shrieking, and Polydorish. No one saw us leave the hotel when, at a late hour, we started on our little excursion. On account of the darkness and the poor landing near the haunted house, we decided to go by the overland route. I managed to purloin a lantern from the kitchen to light our path.

Rob and Beth kept behind Miss Frayne and myself, and in spite of the wildness of the weather, he was evidently pleading his suit, for now and then above the roar of the wind, I heard his ardent voice. Apparently Beth had not yet given him any encouragement.

Going down the lane my lantern underwent a total eclipse, so we had a Jordan-like road to travel. Miss Frayne was quite impervious to unfavorable conditions, as it was a matter of bread and butter to her, she said, and she was accustomed to braving worse storms than this, and anyway she hadn't come here for a summer picnic.

When we came into the grove it was so dark, I lost my bearings.

"Why didn't we bring a flashlight?" asked Beth.

"There were none at the hotel," I told her.

"I know some boys," said Rob with a little laugh, "who would have lent us one—maybe."

Fortunately we were well provided with safety matches and after striking a box or so, we gained the open. A rise of ground hid the house, but when we climbed to the top, the ghost loomed up ghastlier than ever.

I felt the business-like Miss Frayne start and shiver as a little scream escaped her. I didn't wonder. Even I, knowing that it was an illusion and a snare, felt my flesh creeping as I looked at the ghastly thing in the window.

Every now and then according to schedule a light flashed from the windows below. And then came the blood-curdling sounds—whimpers and groans that were rivaling the whistling of the wind.

"This is awful!" said Miss Frayne in a hoarse whisper.

"Do you want to go inside the house?" I asked.

"No—o! I couldn't. Not tonight."

We were some little in advance of Rob and Beth. When one spectral sound came like a tense whisper, Miss Frayne turned and fled, and of course I followed her. We could not see our two companions, but suddenly in an interim of wind and ghost whispers, we heard Beth say:

"Yes, Rob. I think we should really be cosier in a story-and-a-half cottage than we should in a bungalow."

"Ye Gods!" muttered Miss Frayne, "did he propose in the face of that awful Thing?"

"Ship ahoy!" I called.

"Oh, didn't you go inside?" asked Rob.

"Go in! I wouldn't go inside that place; not if I lose my job on the paper. What can it be? You don't seem to mind it, Miss Wade."

"Well, you know," said Beth apologetically, "this is my third performance."

We were now down the hill out of sight of the gruesome, ghastly window display, and Miss Frayne gained courage as we retreated.

"Of course I don't believe in ghosts," she said, "but what do you suppose that is?"

"I had a theory," I said, "that it is the work of a lunatic, but I've since concluded it is due to practical jokers. I'll tell you what I'll do. If you wait here, I'll investigate and see what I can find out for you."

"Oh, would you really dare, Mr. Wade? I don't believe men ever have creepy nerves," she exclaimed.

I began to feel ashamed of my deception.

"I wouldn't go, Lucien," warned Rob, coming to my rescue. "There may be a gang of desperadoes in there, or counterfeit money-makers, or something of that kind. Besides, I have a far more interesting piece of news than anything the ghost could give you."

"Rob!" protested Beth.

"We know it already," I laughed. "It's to be a story-and-a-half high."

"I think I am getting material for quite a story," declared Miss Frayne.

I knew Beth's dislike of scenes and display of emotions—"mock heroics," she called them—so I made no congratulatory speeches of the bless-you-my-children order, but presently under the cover of darkness, I felt a little hand slipped in mine, and my clasp was eloquent of what I felt.

"I hope," said Miss Frayne, "that daylight will make me so ashamed of my cowardice that I can come down here and take some pictures and go inside the house."

"We'll all come with you," promised Beth. "There's safety in numbers."

When we were back at the hotel I managed to have a few words with Rob before we went upstairs.

"Bless the ghost!" he said cheerily. "When Beth first glimpsed it, she just turned and fell into my arms. She was really frightened for the first time. I shall feel under obligations to Ptolemy for a lifetime."

"Thank goodness!" I ejaculated fervently, "that I am under no obligations to a Polydore. Ptolemy certainly did put up the most ghastly thing in the way of ghosts. The lights in the eyes of the skeleton were frightful."

"Did you see the ghost?" asked Silvia sleepily, when I came in.

"Yes; same old ghost, only more of him," I assured her.

She was asleep before I had uttered this reply.

"Silvia," I said, "I have a more startling piece of news for you than that."

She sat bolt upright.

"Are they engaged, Lucien?"

"They are. They are building their castle—I mean their story-and-a-half cottage already."

Alas for my own desire to sleep! I had so effectually awakened Silvia that she planned Beth's trousseau, the wedding, honeymoon, and the furnishing of their house before she subsided.

# XV

# What Miss Frayne Found Out

We had planned to go to the haunted house at nine o'clock the next morning, but owing to my dissipation of the night before, it was long after the appointed hour when Silvia awoke me.

I hurried down stairs and ate my breakfast in solitude. I inquired for Beth and Rob, but the waitress told me they had left the dining-room at seven o'clock and gone for a walk in the woods. She said it with a knowing smile that told me she, too, must be a "sister of the Golden Circle."

"And Miss Frayne?" I asked.

"She went down the road over an hour ago."

Evidently her courage had come up with the sun. I was greatly disturbed at the chance of her stumbling over one or more Polydores, and Rob didn't want to let the cat out of the bag until her article was written, as he believed that if the ghostly spell were broken, she would lose her "punch."

I was unable to think of any plausible explanation to offer Silvia as to why I should start in pursuit, and I wished all sorts of dire calamities on Rob's blond head. Lovers were surely blind and selfish.

About ten o'clock they came strolling in.

"We didn't know it was so late," said Beth cheerfully, "but the boys will keep in the woods all right."

"With her nose for news, there is no telling how far into the woods Miss Frayne's investigation will take her."

"Say we go down by the lane and meet her," proposed Beth, "so that if she has run across the boys we can explain to her why we desire secrecy from Silvia."

"You and Rob go," I advised. "It would seem odd to Silvia if we didn't ask her to go with us."

So the newly engaged couple started down the road, but in their self-absorption they didn't notice the turn to the lane, and they got half way to Windy Creek before they came back to earth and the hotel. Miss Frayne still had not shown up, and I began to have misgivings lest the Polydores had locked her up in the house, but finally just as we were having a happy family gathering and discussing the new event under the shade of the one resort tree, she came excitedly up to us.

"Such an interesting morning as I have had!" she exclaimed enthusiastically. "I made some corking pictures of the place, and I've found out about not only that ghost, but all ghosts—the whole race of ghosts."

I hurriedly interrupted her and made elaborate and jumbled apologies for not keeping our engagement, which evidently bored her and mystified Silvia.

"I am glad I went alone," she finally replied. "Otherwise I might not have got such an interesting interview."

Beth, Rob, and I made frantic and appealing gestures to her behind Silvia's back, but she didn't seem to notice them.

"Whom did you interview, the ghost?" asked Silvia.

"No, indeed. Some very interesting and unusual people who are staying there."

I threw her a wildly beseeching glance and Beth and Rob began at the same time to ply her with distracting questions. I think she seemed to divine that there was something in the situation that was not to be explained, but Silvia interrupted them.

"Do let Miss Frayne tell us about her interview," she said. "We all seem to be very talkative today."

I saw there was no way to dodge the dénouement, so I awaited the finale in dread desperation. It proved to be more of a stunner than I had expected.

"I went down the lane," she said, "and through the grove, up the little hill, and laughed at myself for the hallucinations of the night before. There were no ghosts visible and the door to the haunted house was hospitably open. I stood on the hill long enough to make some pictures and then went on. I walked up the steps fearlessly and looked within. A woman, an untidy, disheveled-looking woman, sat at a table writing furiously in just the same breathless way I write when I have a scoop, and the presses are waiting open-mouthed for my copy.

"She looked up and scowled at my intrusion.

"'Don't bother me,' she said, and continued writing.

"I went through the house and came outside again where I met an absent-minded, spectacled man. I told him who I was and of my object in coming to the house. Then he showed signs of coming to.

"'Oh, the ghost!' he said. 'That is what brought me here. My wife is interested in more tangible, more material things. We have just returned from a long journey, and when we were nearly to our destination, our place of residence, I happened to read in a paper about this haunted house and its apparition, so we came right up here this morning to remain overnight and see if the article were true.'

"I told him how successful I had been and he became quite alert and enthusiastic. He showed me why I should not have been alarmed, because ghosts, he said, were scientific facts. He then explained to me at length how the gases from the dead arise and form a nebulous vapor or a vaporous nebula. It sounded very simple and plausible when he told me, but I can't seem to remember it. Fortunately I have it all down in writing."

Silvia's eyes and mine had met in speechless horror since she had mentioned the "writing woman."

"Lucien!" Silvia now said in a tragic, hoarse whisper—"the Polydores!"

"Oh, do you know them?" asked Miss Frayne. "Dr. Felix Polydore, the eminent LL.D. or something like that."

"The whole family are D's," I said.

"His wife is the highest of high-brows, and they are averse to interviews. They moved to a small city sometime ago to be secluded. Just think of my opportunity! I have them headlined! 'The Haunted House of Hope Haven. Ghost that appears at midnight scientifically explained by the distinguished Dr. Felix Polydore.'"

"I think we are in luck," I said to Silvia, on second thoughts. "We will take them home by the nape of the neck and deliver their children into their keeping to have and to hold."

"I can't turn Diogenes over to them," she said plaintively.

"Diogenes!" repeated Miss Frayne in astonishment.

I then narrated to her the history of our next-door neighbors, and how they planted their five children upon us.

"We had better go down at once and see them," said Silvia, "before they escape. No telling where they might take it in their heads to go."

"We will," I said, "we'll go soon after luncheon."

"Thrice blessed haunted house," quoted Rob. "It gave me Beth, and it has restored the parents of the wise Ptolemy and 'Them Three.'"

"And gave me a ripping story," said Miss Frayne.

Just then the gong sounded, and after luncheon while I was comfortably tipped back in a chair, my feet on the veranda rail, seeing in the smoke from my pipe dream visions of Polydoreless days, a faint cry from Silvia brought me back to earth.

"Lucien, look!"

I looked.

My chair came down to all fours and my feet slipped from the rail.

# XVI

## Ptolemy's Tale

Four defiant, determined-looking Polydores came up the steps and bore down upon us. Then Silvia as usual thought she saw land ahead.

"Oh, boys," she asked hopefully, "did your father send for you to meet him here? And when is he going to take you home?"

"Didn't I tell you," I thundered at Ptolemy, "that you were not to leave that house—"

"It left us," interrupted Emerald with a grin.

"Went up in smoke," added Pythagoras blithely, "ghost and all."

"Four minutes quicker," said Demetrius, "and it would have took father and mother, too."

"Oh, is it the haunted house they are talking about?" asked Miss Frayne joyfully. "What a story I'll have!"

Life to Miss Frayne seemed to be one story after another. Well, it was certainly becoming the same way to us.

"Did the ghost set fire to the house?" asked Beth.

"What are you all talking about," demanded Silvia, "and how did you know these boys were there? How long have you been here?" she asked, turning to Ptolemy.

"I told you," I repeated angrily to the subdued boy, "not to leave. Those were plain orders. If the house did burn up, you could have stayed in your tent in the woods."

Ptolemy's lips twitched faintly.

"The house burned up and all our clothes and our stuff to eat, and our bats and things, and father and mother went away and I didn't know what to do, so—I came here. But we'll go back to our own house. We have learned to cook. Come on, boys."

"You'll stay right here with me, son," and Rob's hand came down intimately on Ptolemy's shoulder.

"It isn't likely we'll turn them out into the woods, when they haven't a roof over their heads," declared Silvia, drawing Emerald to her side.

"I think you are absolutely inhuman, Lucien," cried Beth. "I don't see what has changed you so," and she proceeded to make room for Pythagoras in the porch swing.

"Did the fire scare you?" asked Miss Frayne gently, as she put her arms about Demetrius.

"Et tu, Brute? Well, I plainly see this is no place for an inhuman, childless, married man," I said with a laugh, walking down the veranda.

In the doorway I met Diogenes, who raised his chubby arms invitingly.

"Up, up, Ocean!" he begged sweetly.

I lifted him to my shoulder, and then turned and walked triumphantly back to the family group.

"Now," I said, "here is the whole d-dashed family. And I propose that each keep unto his charge the child he has now under his wing."

Miss Frayne quickly relinquished the dirty Demetrius. Beth shrank away from Pythagoras.

As I seated myself still holding Diogenes, his brothers sprang toward him in greeting, but he spat at one, kicked at another, and pulled the hair of a third, although he patted Ptolemy's cheek gently.

"Now, we'll have this affair thrashed out," I declared in my most authoritative, professional manner, and I then proceeded to explain to Silvia the housing of the Polydores, and our strategies to keep their arrival a secret simply on her account.

"Because you know," interpolated Beth, with a consideration for the feelings of the young Polydores—a consideration they had never before encountered—"we wanted you to have a nice rest."

Silvia looked quite penitent and remorseful for her seeming lack of appreciation of our combined efforts. When I had answered all her inquiries satisfactorily, Miss Frayne's curiosity regarding the progeny of the eminent Polydores had to be fully relieved.

"And do you mean that the scribbling lady I saw at the table is really the mother of these five boys?" she asked, unable to grasp the fact.

"Yes; and the father hereof is the man who explained the ghosts to you so scientifically that you cannot remember what he said. Now, Ptolemy, we'll hear your story of the fire and the whereabouts of your parents. Take your time and tell it accurately."

"Well, you see we did just as you said to, and took the ghost out of the window and went out to the woods early this morning so as not to let the paper lady see us."

"Oh!" cried Miss Frayne, "am I the paper lady? I begin to see daylight. Are these boys the ghost perpetrators, and were you in on the put-up job?"

"You're a good guesser," I replied.

"And why wasn't I taken into your confidence?"

"For two reasons. First, because your friend Rob said you'd get better results for copy—more inspirations and thrills, if you weren't behind the scenes on the ghost business—and then we didn't want to tell you about the presence of the Polydores lest inadvertently you betray the fact to my wife. Now, proceed, Ptolemy."

"After we were in the woods, I heard an automobile coming down the lane, and I went up near the edge of the woods and peeked out behind a tree, and pretty soon I saw father and mother come over the hill and go in our haunted house, so I came up there and hid under the window and heard mother say: 'What an ideal place to write this is. It looks as if I might really get a chance to write unmo—'

"'—lested,'" I finished for him.

"I guess so," he allowed. "Well, she began writing, so I didn't go in, but when father came outside I went up to him and told him you and mudder were at the hotel and that we

were all with you. He told me they came up here to write
an article for some big magazine about the ghost. He hired
an automobile down at Windy Creek to bring them up to
the house and the man was going to come back for them
tomorrow morning. I didn't let on the ghost was a fake,
because I thought he'd be so disappointed to have all his
trouble for nothing, and he'd be mad at me for swiping his
skull. I told him a paper lady was coming and then I went
back to the woods. He went down with me to see the boys,
and he said he would come back and have lunch with us.
Mother doesn't ever stop to eat at noon when she is writing.

"He went back and talked to the paper lady and pretty
soon he came down and ate with us. I told him all about
how we couldn't get any girl to do the work for us and so we
had been living with you, and how Di got sick and mudder
was all worn out taking care of him and came down here to
rest, and that you wouldn't cash the check, so I did and was
spending it and he said that was all right." Here Ptolemy
flashed me a most triumphant glance.

"He said you must be paid for all your expense and
trouble, so he made out a check and gave it to me and told
me to make mudder a nice present. He ain't so bad when he
ain't thinking about dead stuff. When he felt in his pocket
for his check book, he found a letter he had got yesterday
and forgotten to open, so he read it then and found it was
from some magazine, and the man said he'd pay his and
mother's expenses to go to Chili and write up some stuff
about—something. So father said they must go at once."

"Not to Chili!" I exclaimed.

"Yes; we all went up to the house with him and I took mother's pencil and paper away so she would have to listen. She was wild for Chili, and I had to go and hunt up a farmer who had a machine to take them down to Windy Creek. Father signed another blank check for you and said you could board us with it or do anything you thought best.

"Then mother took a lot of papers out of her bag, some stuff she had written and didn't get suited with, and she stuffed them in the stove and set fire to them. Then we all went down to the lane to see father and mother off and when we got back the house was on fire. The chimney burned out."

"Guess mother must have written some hot stuff," said Emerald.

"It was burning so fast," continued Ptolemy, "that we didn't dast go in to save anything and all our food and clothes and balls and bats and fishing tackle are gone, and we didn't know what to do, or what to eat, and so—we came here."

"You did just right, Ptolemy," I admitted. "I shouldn't have called you down—not until I heard your story, anyway."

I held out my hand, which he shook solemnly, but with an injured air.

"Do you mean to tell me," asked Miss Frayne, "that your father and mother went away without seeing the baby?"

Ptolemy flushed a little.

"You see," he explained apologetically, "mother gets woolly when she writes and she's forgotten there's Di. She thinks Demetrius is the youngest. She's mad about writing. If she sees a blank paper anywhere, she ain't happy until she has written something on it, and the sight of a pencil makes her fingers itch."

"Take warning, Miss Frayne," I said, "and don't get too literary."

"Some day," resumed Ptolemy, "mother'll get the antiques all out of her system and then she'll remember us."

I liked the boy's defense of his mother, and I began to see that Rob was right in thinking there were possibilities in the lad, but it was Silvia's influence that had developed them, for in the days when he borrowed soup plates of us, there had been no redeeming trait that I could discern.

And while I was recalling this, I heard Silvia saying to him kindly: "And in the meantime, I'll be 'mudder' to you."

"So will I," chimed in Beth.

"I'll be a big brother," offered Rob.

"I'll be next friend, Ptolemy," I contributed.

Strange to say, my offer seemed to make the most impression on him. He came to me and gazed into my eyes earnestly.

"I'll do just as you say," he promised.

"Where do we'uns come in?" asked Pythagoras, with one of his satanic grins.

Miss Frayne saved the day.

"You all come in with me," she said, "and have lunch. I haven't eaten since breakfast, and I understand there is warm ginger cake and huckleberry pie. Aren't you hungry?"

"You bet," spoke up Pythagoras. "We only had coffee, peanuts, and beans down in the woods, and father ate the beans and drank all the coffee."

"We're out of the frying pan into the fire," said Silvia woefully, when we were alone.

"I wish the Polydore parents had gone up in smoke," I declared.

"Then your last hope of getting rid of the children would have gone up in smoke, too," argued Beth.

"No; in case of the demise of their parents, we could have turned them over body and soul to the probate court," I informed her.

"We will fill out this blank check for any amount, Lucien," declared Silvia, "that will induce a housekeeper to take charge of their house. I shall keep Diogenes, though, until he is older."

"I wouldn't mind Ptolemy, either," I admitted. "I shall be interested in seeing what I can make of him, and he hasn't a bad influence over Diogenes, but I'll be hanged if anything would induce me to have 'Them Three' Chessy cats running wild over us. They can live in their house alone, or be put in a reformatory. We won't have them. We're under no obligations, pecuniary or moral, to look after them."

"I think, Lucien, we might as well go home now. We've had a good rest and a good time, and I am anxious to be back and see how Huldah is getting on."

As Huldah had never mastered two of the three R's, we had not been able to receive any reports from her.

"I'll tell you what we'll do," proposed Beth. "Rob and I will take all the Polydores save Diogenes, and go home tomorrow and prepare the house and Huldah for the overflow. Then you two can come on with Diogenes the next day."

"Good idea, Beth!" I approved. "I'd hate to face Huldah, unprepared, with the return of the Polydores *en masse.*"

"I am glad," said Silvia, "that Huldah has been having a rest from them for a few days."

# XVII

## All About
## Uncle Issachar's Visit

The next morning's stage carried seven passengers to Windy Creek, as Miss Frayne with a big roll of "copy" also took her departure.

Diogenes had been quite docile and amenable to my rule since the licking I gave him, so we had a pleasant and comfortable return journey on the following day.

"I hope, Lucien," said Silvia, "you won't refuse to cash this check for a good amount. The Polydore parents may never show up, and it's only right we should be reimbursed for their keep."

"I will cash it," I assured her, "and use it for a housekeeper or else send the boys off to a school. I should like very much to have it out with Felix Polydore, but, as you suggest, I may never have the opportunity to see him at close range."

Beth, Rob, and Ptolemy met us at the station.

"Where are 'Them Three'?" I asked hopefully.

"Huldah is feeding them little pies hot from the kettle—the kind she cooks like doughnuts, you know."

"Huldah cooking for 'Them Three'!" I exclaimed. "She must have passed into her second childhood. She grudged them even an apple to piece on."

"She has pampered them ever since our return," said Rob.

"Poor Huldah! She must indeed be afflicted with softening of the brain," I decided.

"She has probably been so lonely, shut in here by herself," said Silvia, "that even 'Them Three' looked good to her."

In the hallway Huldah met us. She was beaming with pleasure, but except in her bearing toward the children, she was quite normal.

"We've all had a real good rest," she observed, "and you do look so well, Mrs. Wade. My! but this place has been lonesome. I'm glad we're all together again."

"Now, Silvia, shut your eyes," directed Beth, "and come into the library. Ptolemy has bought you a present with the check his father gave him."

"Beth helped me pick it out," said Ptolemy.

Beth led the way into the library, and we followed.

"Open your eyes."

Silvia gave a little cry of pleasure, and looking over her shoulder, I beheld a baby grand piano.

"Oh, Ptolemy!" she cried, giving him a fervent kiss and fond hug, "I can never let you do so much."

"Oh, yes," he said, flushing a little under the endearments which were doubtless the first ever bestowed upon him. "Father's got a whole lot of money grandpa left him and it's fixed so he can't draw out only so much each year. He said the board and bother of us was worth more than this and we'll all enjoy the music. But Thag and Em and Dem ain't to touch it. I'll knock tar out of the first one that comes near it."

I was disconsolate. I didn't see how we could return it and I didn't want the Polydore web woven any tighter. To think of Silvia's receiving from them what it had been my longing to give her! But as I was to learn later, she was to acquire much more than a piano from the eminent family.

After dinner Silvia asked Huldah to come in and hear the music, and when Silvia's repertoire was exhausted, we gave our faithful servant all the little details of our trip which Beth had not supplied.

"Now tell us, Huldah, how things went along here," said Silvia.

"Well, you think some wonderful things happened to you all on your trip mebby—ghosts and proposals," looking at Beth and Rob, "and fires and Polydores, but back here in this quiet house something happened that has your ghosts and things skinned by a mile."

"Oh, dear!" cried Silvia apprehensively, "what is it?"

"Break it very gently, Huldah," I cautioned. "You know we've borne a good deal."

"Your uncle Issachar was here for a couple of days."

She certainly had made a sensation.

"Not Uncle Issachar! Not here?" exclaimed Silvia incredulously.

"Yes, ma'am. He came the next day after Beth and Mr. Rossiter and Polly left. I told him you'd gone away for a little vacation and rest. I didn't let on that I knew where you had gone, because I didn't want him straggling up there, too, or sending for you to come back. He said your absence would make no difference to his plans; that he never let nothing do that. He come to pay a visit and he should pay one."

"Yes," said Silvia feebly. "That sounds like Uncle Issachar."

"I told him to make himself perfectly at home; that every one did that to this place, and he said he would. I'd just slicked up the big front room upstairs and I seen to it that he had everything all right. I cooked the best dinner I knew how, and he said it was the first white man's meal he had eat since his ma died, so I found out what she used to cook and fed him on it. Them three kids and him eat like they was holler. I guess if Polly hadn't took them away your grocery bill would 'a looked like Barb'ry Allen's grave.

"Well, as I was saying, your uncle he eat till he got over his grouches, and like enough he'd be here eating yet, if he hadn't got a telegraph to hit the line for home, some big business deal, he said, and I guess it was a great deal, for he licked his chops and smacked his lips over it, and he give me a ten dollar bill to get a new dress and each of Them Three one dollar fer candy."

"The old tightwad!" I exclaimed. "It was your cooking, sure, that made him loosen up that way."

"Tightwad nothing!" she declared indignantly. "You won't think he was tight-wadded when you read this here letter he left for you. He told me what was in it, and I've just been busting to tell it to Beth, but I waited for you to know it first."

With great excitement Silvia opened the letter, read it, gasped, re-read it, and then in consternation handed it to me.

"Read it aloud, Lucien," she bade. "Maybe I can believe it then."

This was the letter.

"My dear Niece:

"I was sorry not to see you, but glad to learn that, as every wise and good woman should do, you are raising a fine family—a family of *sons*, which is what our country most needs. Your son Pythagoras informed me that you had taken your oldest child, Ptolemy, and your youngest, Diogenes, with you, I am glad you left three such promising samples for me to see.

"As you have five sons, I have, agreeable to my promise, placed in your name in the First National Bank of your city the sum of twenty-five thousand dollars.

"Your affectionate uncle,<br>
"Issachar Innes."

"Huldah," I asked, "did you tell him the Polydores were our children?"

"Me?" she repeated indignantly. "Me tell a lie like that! No; I didn't get no chance to tell him anything about them. 'Them Three' done the telling. The first thing that one"—pointing to Pythagoras—"said was, 'Mudder went away and took the baby, Diogenes, with her.' And then that next one"—indicating Emerald—"said: 'Yes, and our oldest brother, Ptolemy, went on with Beth to see them.'

"The old gent asked them all their names and ages and he was so pleased and said he thought it was just fine for you to raise five sons, so I didn't have no heart to tell him no different. 'Twan't none of my business anyhow. Then 'Them Three' kept talking about stepdaddy, and your Uncle Issachar asks 'Who the devil is he? Did my niece marry again?' And I told him as how Mr. Wade was all the husband you ever had, and that stepdaddy was nothing but a sort of pet-name the kids had give Mr. Wade."

"I told him," said Demetrius, "that stepdaddy was cross to us sometimes and not as nice as mudder, and he said—"

"You shut up," commanded Huldah quickly, "and let me talk."

"No," I intercepted, "I'd really be interested in hearing what he told Uncle Issachar. What was it, Demetrius, that your great-uncle said to you?"

"He said," stated the imp, darting his tongue out in triumph at his victory over Huldah, "that he always thought you was a stiff."

"He didn't say nothing of the kind!" declared Huldah. "He said you was stiff-necked, and that he presumed you would act more like a stepfather than the real thing. Well, as I was saying, he asked their names, and he liked them fine. Said they were so classy."

"Didn't he say classic, Huldah?" inquired Rob.

"Mebby. What's the difference?" snapped Huldah.

"None," I assured her quickly, dodging a definition.

"She told him—" began Emerald.

"You shut up," again adjured Huldah, "or I'll never bake you one of those small pies no more."

"Oh, please, Huldah," I coaxed. "Let us hear everything. I've always told you my life's secrets, and I don't mind what you or the boys told him."

"Well, I suppose what he was going to tattle was that I thought the old gent might feel hurt, 'cause none of them was named after him, so I told him Polly's middle name was Issachar."

"Why, Huldah," remonstrated Silvia.

"Well, he's always wanted a middle name, and he's never been baptized, so you can stick it in and have him ducked next Sunday and then that will square that. 'Them Three' stuck to him like a hive of bees, and I was scairt for fear they'd let the cat out of the bag, and so long as they had put it in, I thought it might just as well stay in, but they were just as slick as grease in all they said. They'll hang in that rogues' gallery yet."

"I suppose they were pretty—strenuous," said Silvia with a sigh.

"They was more than that. The first afternoon right after dinner when he was sitting on the front porch, sleeping peaceful and snoring, that there one—" pointing to Pythagoras—

"Tattle-tale!" he began, but I administered a cuff and he subsided into surprised silence.

"He," said Huldah, looking pleased at this little attention to the boy, "went to the front window and dropped a young kitten down on the old gent's head. It clawed something fierce. We had just got things going smooth again when Emmy got one of his earaches. I roasted an onion and put it in his ear, and what did he do but take it out of his ear and slip it down your poor uncle's back."

"Why didn't you beat them?" I asked indignantly.

"Because the old gent did that. He put 'em across his knee, and believe me, it was some licking they caught. They didn't let out a whimper and that pleased him."

"Huh!" said Emerald. "Thag don't know how to cry. He hasn't got any tears, and old Uncle Iz didn't hurt me, because, you see, when I heard Thag getting his, I went and stuffed the Declaration of Independence, that book of stepdaddy's that Demetrius tore the pictures out of, in my pants."

"Go on!" urged Rob delightedly. "What else did you all do? Uncle must have had some time. It would make a fine scenario. 'The first visit of the rich uncle.'"

"Well," resumed Huldah. "One of 'em put red pepper in the old man's bed, and he like to sneeze his head off, but he said as how sneezing was healthy, and showed you'd got rid of a cold."

"He went to the front window and dropped a kitten down on the
old gent's head."

"He never got on to the pepper," said Demetrius gleefully.

"In the morning, that second one put a toad in his new uncle's pocket, and Emmy broke his specs. Then Meetie he dropped his watch. They used his razor to cut the lawn with. And then they took him down to the creek to go fishing, and they put the fish in Uncle's silk hat, and—"

"Stop!" implored Silvia, who was now in tears. "Uncle Issachar believes them mine! Ours! And that I brought them up! Oh, why did we ever go away?"

"Oh, pshaw," exclaimed Huldah comfortingly, "he said you had brung them up fine; that they were no mollycoddles or Lizzie boys, and he didn't suppose you had so much sense as to leave them natural."

"A left-handed one for mudder," laughed Beth.

"He must be a very peculiar man—ready for the asylum, I should say," commented Rob.

"He would have been if he'd stayed any longer, or else I would have been," declared Huldah.

"Couldn't you make them behave, someway?" asked Silvia.

"Well, at first I tried to, and every time I pinched one of 'em when the old gent wasn't looking, or knocked 'em down when I got 'em alone, they would threaten to tell who they was, and then when I seen how your uncle liked the way they acted, I just let 'em go it, head on. And seeing as how they each brung you five thousand, I've treated 'em best I know how. They're worth it, now. They done one thing more that was awful. Could you stand it to hear?" turning to Silvia.

"Please, Silvia," implored Rob.

"Well," argued Silvia faintly. "I suppose we might as well know the worst."

"You see the old gent didn't always get up to breakfast with the kids and one morning when I brought in the cakes Emmy looked up and grinned. I nearly dropped the plate. He had both sets of the old man's false teeth in his mouth. I got 'em back in his room without his waking, but I'd have liked a picture of Emmy."

"Pythagoras," I demanded, when we had recovered from this recital, "why didn't you tell him who you were, and how you all came to be here with us?"

"Because she is our mudder, and we are going to stay with her, always. We've got a snap. So has father and mother. And Ptolemy told us that if you ever got any kids, you'd get five thousand each for them, and I thought we'd just make that much for you. So we played Uncle Iz for it. Easy money, all right, all right."

"Talk about fine financiering," quoth Rob. "'Them Three' will surely land on Wall Street."

But poor Silvia had no heart for humor and was weeping silently.

"Why, look here, my dear," I said in consolation, "this is a very simple matter to adjust. In the morning when you feel better, just write a full explanation of the affair and inclose your check for twenty-five thousand."

Silvia quickly wiped away her tears.

"I'll do it tonight, Lucien. I feel better now. I never thought of writing."

Huldah and "Them Three" looked most lugubrious.

"The old skinflint won't miss it as much as I would a penny," declared our faithful handmaiden. "And I'm sure you've earnt that twenty-five thousand if anyone ever did. You've had as much care and worry about them brats as you would if they'd been your own."

"Huldah," I said severely, "there is a pretty stiff penalty for obtaining money under false pretences."

"After all the pains we took to make things lively for him, so he wouldn't get bored and think he was having a poor time!" regretted Pythagoras.

"And us watching every word we spoke so as not to give it away," wailed Emerald.

"Cake's all dough," muttered Demetrius.

Ptolemy regarded the three disapprovingly. He had the old inscrutable look, the look that foreboded mischief, in his eyes.

"You bungled, you fool kids!" he said in disgust, "and Huldah, what did you want to let on to mudder for that he thought we was hers? You ought to have torn up the note he left and just said he'd put twenty-five thousand in the bank for her."

"Huh! you're just jealous because you weren't in the Uncle Izzy deal yourself," jeered Pythagoras. "You always think you're the only one that can do anything right."

"I wish you had been here, Polly," said Huldah, "I am sure you could have worked it through somehow."

"I wish I had stayed and put it across," he answered. "If you and the kids would only learn not to blab everything you know. It's the only way to work anything. Minute you tell a thing, it's all off."

There was still a great deal of development work to be put on Ptolemy's moral standard.

"You'll find, my lad," remonstrated Rob, "that honesty is the best policy."

"I'd have been perfectly honest about it," he defended. "I would have told him the truth, and how our parents had deserted us, and how mudder took us in when we were homeless and was bringing us up like her own because she hadn't got any, and how stepdaddy wanted to turn us out, and she wouldn't let him, and then he would have decided against stepdaddy and given mudder the money so she could keep us."

"Ptolemy," I said warningly, "there is a way of telling the truth, or rather of coloring white lies with enough truth to make them deceive, that is more dishonorable than an out and out lie."

"Tell me, Ptolemy," asked Silvia, "how did you know about that offer of five thousand dollars for each child?"

"I overheard it," he said guardedly, "but I can't remember where."

"He heard me say so," confessed Huldah.

"It was when he first come here and he was making us so much trouble, and I told him it was too bad we had to have other folks' brats around when, if we only had our own, they'd be bringing in something."

The recital now broke up and Silvia sat down to write a long explanatory letter to Uncle Issachar. The next morning I procured her a check from the First National Bank and she filled it out.

"Oh!" she said with indrawn breath, when she had asked me how to write twenty-five thousand dollars, "I never expected to be able to sign my name to a check for such an amount."

"You never will again, I fear," was my sad prophecy.

"It must feel rich," said Beth, "just to have a large check pass through your fingers."

"Them Three" came the nearest to tears that they were able to do.

"We worked so hard for it," they sighed.

"So did I!" muttered Huldah.

"I couldn't live a double life," declared Silvia.

# XVIII

## In Which I Decide on Extreme Measures

Everyone in our house, which was now filled to overflowing—in fact, there were Polydores on sofas and in beds on the floor—save Silvia and myself, was on the alert for a response to the letter during the succeeding few days. Knowing Uncle Issachar, we felt sure he would make no response, or notice the matter in any way save to cash the check promptly.

The monotony was somewhat relieved by the difficulties under which Beth and Rob were pursuing their courtship. On the third evening succeeding our return, Silvia and I started upstairs early to give them a chance to have the exclusive use of the library, the Polydores having all been sent to bed. As we were making some plausible excuse for going to our room, Beth remarked with a smile:

"Your motive in retiring so early is commendable, but of no particular benefit to Rob and me. The Polydores, like the poor, we always have with us."

"I saw that every one of them except Ptolemy was in bed at eight o'clock last night and the night before," said Silvia. "You don't mean to tell me—"

"Yes, I do mean," laughed Beth. "Not Ptolemy, though. He has become too dignified to spy on us, but last night as we sat here on the settee, we heard a suppressed sneeze, and Rob pulled Emerald from underneath."

"How in the world did he ever squeeze under there?" I asked, gazing at the slight space between the floor and settee.

"He did look a little flattened, as if he had been put in a letter press," said Rob. "I gave him a dime to go to bed and stay there. Beth and I had just resumed our conversation when a still, small voice said: 'I'll go to bed for a dime, too.' I then hauled Demetrius from behind the davenport."

"And the night before," said Beth, "when we were sitting on the porch, Pythagoras rolled off the roof, where he had been listening to us, and came down into the vines."

"Now I'll stop that," I declared. "I'll tie them in their beds and lock the doors and windows."

"No," refused Rob. "I'd like to try to circumvent them by their own weapons of wits. I have a little plan which I don't dare whisper to you lest their long-range ears get in their work. We are just about to start for a walk."

"In this pouring rain!" protested Silvia.

"We like the rain," he replied, "and we—are not going far."

Pythagoras entered the room just then and looked astounded and disappointed when he saw Beth and Rob departing.

"We are going out to a small party," Rob remarked to me, casually.

It was after eleven when we heard them returning.

"Do you suppose they have been walking all this time?" said Silvia in concern. "Beth wore no rubbers."

The next day was Sunday and Huldah put into execution a plan for procuring one happy hour each week. This plan was the admission of the Polydores, *en masse*, to one of the Sunday schools. She chose the church most remote from home so they would be a long time going and coming, which she said would "help some."

"Now," said Beth, as she watched them march away, "I can dare to tell you where we spent last evening. We were at the Polydore house next door. There is a little vine-screened porch on the other side of the house. Rob managed to open one of the windows and brought out a couple of chairs. It was as snug as could be."

"I'll corral them every night," I said, "until you make your getaway, and I'll give you the key so you can go inside when it is cool or stormy."

"We'll go around the block by way of precaution," said Rob.

Presently Huldah returned from the Sunday school with triumphant mien.

"They made them all into one class and put a redheaded woman with spectacles in for their teacher. I gave them street car tickets to come home on."

When the Polydores returned, however, they were dragging Diogenes along and he looked quite weary.

"Didn't you come home on the street car?" I asked Ptolemy.

"No; we sold our tickets and got ice cream sodas," he explained. "We took turns carrying Diogenes on our backs."

"You only had one ticket for yourself, and two half fares for Thag and Emmy," said Huldah suspiciously. "I thought Meetie and Di could ride free. You couldn't have sold them tickets for enough for sodies."

"Rob gave us three nickels to put in the plate," said Pythagoras. "We only put in one of them, seeing we were all in one family and one class. That gave us four nickels for ice cream sodas and the clerk gave Di half a glass some one had left."

"I gave you a penny for Di to put in," said Huldah. "What did you do with that?"

"We wanted him to put it in, and when they took up the collection, he wouldn't give it," said Emerald. "I tried to take it away from him and he swallowed it. The redhead teacher was awful scared, but I told her he was used to swallowing things and that you said he carried a whole department store in his insides."

"Poor little Di," said Silvia; "it's the only way he has of keeping things away from you all."

That night I saw to it personally that each and every Polydore was in his little bed. It should have aroused my suspicions that none of them rebelled, or had evinced the slightest degree of interest or curiosity when Beth and Rob announced their intention of going out for the evening.

At ten-thirty the lovers returned, bringing in Pythagoras, who was clad in his pajamas.

"Where did you pick him up?" I asked in astonishment.

"He picked us up," said Beth.

"He was wise, maybe, in discovering where we were," said Rob, "but he fell down when he tried to work off the ghost screeches on us. We recognized them at once, and ran him down inside, so our party broke up."

"Come here, Pythagoras," I commanded.

He obeyed promptly and fearlessly.

"How did you know they were there, and when did you go over there?"

"I was playing over in our house today," he replied, "and I found one of Beth's hairpins with the little stones in, in the big chair, so I knew that was where they hid last night. As soon as you went down stairs tonight, I got out the window and slid down the roof and came over to scare them."

"You've missed a lot of sleep the last few nights," I said quietly, "so you will have to make it up. You can stay in bed all day to-morrow."

"Hold on, Lucien!" exclaimed Rob. "Tomorrow's the big baseball game of the season, and I promised to take them all."

"So much the better," I said. "He will learn to mind."

Pythagoras looked as if he had been struck, and quickly put his arms across his eyes. In a moment his shoulders were heaving. At last I had found a vulnerable spot in the stoic, and I began to relent.

"See here, Pythagoras," I said, "if I let you up in time to go to the game, will you promise me something?"

"Anything," came in a muffled voice.

"Will you promise not to spy on Beth and Rob and keep Emerald and Demetrius from doing it?"

"Yes," he promised quickly, his arm coming down and his face brightening. "Sure I will, but I did want to hear what they said."

"Why?" asked Rob interestedly.

"We're getting up a show, and Em is going to take the part of a girl and he spoons with Tolly, and we didn't know what to have them say to each other."

"I'll rehearse you on the play, and prompt you," said Beth with a little giggle.

"Come on upstairs with me now," I said to Pythagoras.

When I landed him at his door, he leaned up against me, and rubbed his cheek against my arm.

"Thank you for letting me go to the game," he said.

I found myself responding to his affectionate advance. This would clearly never do. I couldn't let another Polydore squeeze himself into my regard.

"Silvia," I said abruptly, as I came into our room, "we must really make some immediate plan for disposing of the Polydores, or, at least, of 'Them Three.'"

"Huldah is managing them tolerably well," demurred Silvia. "Since they depreciated in market value from five thousand per to nothing, she has resumed her former harsh treatment of them."

"Well, we are not going to keep them," I replied with finality. "We are under no obligations to do so. I am going to put them in a school for boys and use the blank check Felix Polydore left to pay for their tuition."

"I suppose that is what we will have to do," she admitted with a little sigh. "Yet, Lucien, it doesn't seem quite right. If they are in a boys' school, they will keep on right along the same lines. They need home influence and contact with women. Demetrius is fond of music and will sit still and listen when I play. Emerald obeyed me to-day the first time I spoke, and I even thought I saw a glimmer of good in Pythagoras."

I didn't tell her that this glimmer was what had decided me to dispose of him.

"It would, doubtless, be better for them to stay," I admitted, "but I am not going to be a martyr to the cause. They are going."

The next morning I wrote for catalogues and prospectus to the different schools, and I felt as if three old men of the sea had been lifted from my shoulders.

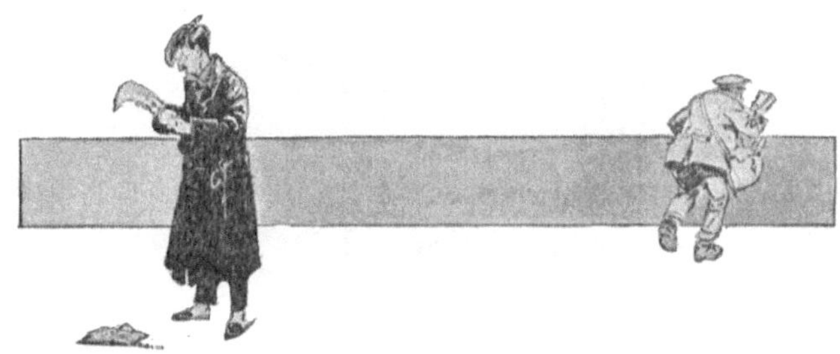

# XIX

## Which Has to Do with Some Letters

One morning when I came down to my office, I found a letter postmarked from the city in which Uncle Issachar lived addressed to me. I opened it and found inclosed, with seal unbroken, the letter Silvia had mailed to her uncle and which she had marked "personal." There was a note addressed to me accompanying it:

"Dear Sir:

"I am returning herewith your personal letter to Mr. Innes, as he has gone to South America and left no forwarding address. Should such be received from him at any future date, you will be duly notified thereof.

"Very truly yours,<br>
"Chester K. Winslow,<br>
"Secretary."

I read the above to Silvia at luncheon. She was grievously disappointed because her uncle had not received her letter of explanation.

"It is most fortunate," she said, "that I sent it in one of your office envelopes."

As usual, she had found the bright spot she always looked for and generally discovered.

"I wouldn't care," she said, "to have Uncle Issachar's private secretary or the dead-letter office know all our private affairs, but I shall feel like an impostor until Uncle Issachar is undeceived."

"I feel a hunch," said Rob, "that Uncle Issachar will run across Doctor Felix and his wife down there in Chili and find you out."

"He may run across the Polydores," I replied, "but he'll never find out from them that they are the parents of Silvia's children. They would not mention a subject in which they have so little interest."

"But," argued Beth, "naturally they'd tell him where they lived, and then, of course, he'd say he had a niece living in the same town. They would inquire her name and inform him that they were her near neighbors, and then he'd tell them what fine sons you have, and then, of course, the Polydores would claim their own."

"Which theory goes to show," said Silvia, "how little you know Uncle Issachar and the Polydore seniors. He would not think of speaking to strangers, and if he did, he wouldn't say any of those usual conversational things you mentioned. The Polydores wouldn't be interested, in the least, in knowing he had a niece unless she happened to know something about antiques, and if he should describe her children, she wouldn't recognize them."

After luncheon I went out on the porch. While I sat there, the mail carrier came along and handed me a letter—a returned letter. It was directed in Ptolemy's round hand to Mr. Issachar Innes. He had evidently used the envelope to Silvia's letter to her uncle as his model, for the address was written in the same way. "Personal" was added in the left-hand corner, and his name and our house number was in the upper left-hand corner.

I went into the library where my wife, Beth, Rob, and Ptolemy were sitting.

"Ptolemy," I said, handing him the letter, "here is your communication to Uncle Issachar, returned."

He lost some of his usual *sang froid* and appeared quite disconcerted.

"Why, Ptolemy," exclaimed Silvia in consternation, "what in the world did you write to Uncle Issachar about?"

Ptolemy had recovered and was quite himself again.

"About us," he said innocently. "As the oldest of our family, I thought I ought to do a little explaining."

"And I think," I said, looking at him keenly, "that we have the right to know what your explanation was."

Ptolemy handed me over the letter.

"Read it aloud," he said, with the air of one who is proud of his productions.

Rob's eyes shone in anticipation.

I broke the seal. A note from the secretary fell out. It was an apology for not returning the letter sooner, but it had been inadvertently mislaid. I then read aloud the letter Ptolemy had written:

"Dear Uncle Issachar

"I am sorry Diogenes and I were away when you were here. You thought the others were fine, but you should have seen—Diogenes. I hope you will send mudder back her check, because there is lots of things she needs, and it takes a lot of money to take care of all us. You see our own father and mother don't want to be bothered with us and they went away and left us, and so we are living with mudder the same as if we were really her adopted children, and if her own would have been worth five thousand per to you, I think her adopted children ought to be worth half as much anyway, so it would only be fair to send her a check for $12,500 anyway, and if you are a good sport like the kids said you were, you'll send back her check.

"Yours truly,
"P. Issachar Polydore Wade."

Rob's laughter was so free and spontaneous that I had to join in against my will. Ptolemy, who had seemed a little apprehensive of the verdict, looked accordingly relieved.

"That's a fine letter, young man," approved Rob. "Stepdaddy ought to take you into his law firm."

"No," declared Beth. "I think Ptolemy has inherited his mother's gift. He should be a writer."

"Not on your life!" cried Ptolemy with feeling. "I want to live things instead of writing about them."

A tear or two came into Silvia's eyes.

"It was very sweet in you, Ptolemy, to try to get the money for mudder."

I felt that all this commendation was bad for Ptolemy, and that it was up to me to take a reef in his sails.

"It was a well-meant letter, Ptolemy," I said, "and I know that your motive was unselfish, but it is very poor policy to meddle in other people's affairs. Meddlers are mischief makers in spite of their good intentions. I am very glad it did not fall into Uncle Issachar's hands."

Ptolemy looked sufficiently squelched.

"By the way, Silvia," I said. "I wrote Mr. Winslow and told him not to forget to forward Uncle Issachar's address as soon as he possibly could do so, as I had matters of importance to communicate to him."

"He may travel about like father and mother," said Ptolemy, again regaining confidence, "so why don't you put that check for twenty-five thousand in the Savings Department and get the interest on it anyway?"

"I think, Ptolemy," said Rob, "that you are too good a financier, after all, to become a lawyer. I will go back to my first conviction that you should be a promoter."

"We'll give him to Uncle Issachar," I proposed, "for a partner."

# XX

## "The Money We Earnt for You"

Life went on uneventfully save for the dire doings of "Them Three." Knowing that they were to be sent to school, they were having their last fling at life untrammeled. September came, and Rob set the day for his departure, as he was going home to arrange his affairs, so he and Beth could leave for an extended honeymoon trip. I planned to go with Rob and install the Polydore three in their distant school. They were so despondent at leaving, as the time drew near, that a feeling of gloom hung over the household, all the members of which, even to Huldah, urged me to relent. But I remained adamant until the evening before the day set for the dissolution of the Polydore family, when something happened that changed all our plans.

We were assembled in the library in a state of forced cheerfulness when the doorbell rang. I answered it, and receipted for a telegram which I opened and read in the hall. It was from Chester K. Winslow.

"Silvia," I said gravely, as I returned to the library, "your Uncle Issachar is dead. Died in South America. Heart disease. Very sudden."

Conflicting emotions were depicted in Silvia's expression.

The thought uppermost in all our minds was expressed simultaneously by "Them Three."

"Gee! Then you can keep the money we earnt for you."

"You know," interpolated Rob in soft-pedaled tone, "they are going to train school children toward the military—teach the young ideas how to shoot, as it were. It won't be long before they are ordered to Mexico to protect us."

"If Them Three ever meets that there Viller man," commented Huldah confidently, "the fur will fly some."

"Lucien," said Silvia thoughtfully, "we are under obligations to these children, you see, after all."

"Yes," I acknowledged with a sigh, "seeing they are now ours, bought and paid for, I suppose we'll have to treat them as such."

"You wouldn't send your own kids away to school," said Pythagoras significantly.

"No," I reluctantly allowed, answering the protest of Pythagoras, "and we won't send you. You will all go to the public school tomorrow."

The deafening Polydore powwow that followed made me hope that Uncle Issachar had met with his just deserts.

## About the Author

Belle Kanaris Maniates was born in 1860 in Marshall, Michigan. Her father, Nicholas Maniates, a Greek immigrant, died when she was 9 months old, leaving her mother Martha to support Belle and her three siblings. Maniates was a prolific writer in the early twentieth century, publishing hundreds of short stories and eight books. Many of her novels were aimed at juvenile audiences and addressed issues of orphans and immigrant life.

Maniates never married, instead supporting herself as a writer and as a clerk at the Michigan state capitol for 30 years. She died in 1931 at the age of 70.